Love Double Dutch!

Love
Double

Dutch!

Doreen Spicer-Dannelly

RANDOM HOUSE New York

Text copyright © 2018 by Doreen Spicer-Dannelly
Jacket art copyright © 2018 by Vanessa Brantley Newton

All rights reserved. Published in the United States by Random House Children's Books, a division of Penguin Random House LLC, New York.

Random House and the colophon are registered trademarks of Penguin Random House LLC.

Visit us on the Web! rhcbooks.com

Educators and librarians, for a variety of teaching tools, visit us at RHTeachersLibrarians.com

Library of Congress Cataloging-in-Publication Data
Names: Spicer-Dannelly, Doreen, author.
Title: Love Double Dutch! / by Doreen Spicer-Dannelly.
Description: First edition. | New York : Random House, [2017] | Summary: "Kayla must salvage her double Dutch dreams after her parents' rocky relationship takes her away from Brooklyn—and her beloved team—to spend the summer in North Carolina" —Provided by publisher.
Identifiers: LCCN 2016028497 | ISBN 978-1-5247-0000-3 (hardcover) | ISBN 978-1-5247-0002-7 (ebook) | ISBN 978-1-5247-0001-0 (hardcover library binding)
Subjects: | CYAC: Rope skipping—Fiction. | Family problems—Fiction. | African Americans—Fiction. | Family life—North Carolina—Fiction. | North Carolina—Fiction.
Classification: LCC PZ7.1.S7145 Lov 2017 | DDC [Fic]—dc23

Printed in the United States of America
10 9 8 7 6 5 4 3 2 1
First Edition

Random House Children's Books
supports the First Amendment and celebrates the right to read.

Contents

Double the Pressure

*M*an, *it's hot!* The air is thick and sticky like the lotion on my skin, and it's just the way I like Brooklyn in the summertime. People around Bed-Stuy are always complaining about the humidity, but I love it. It's like drinking water when I'm jumping double Dutch. Refreshing. But one thing I can't stand is when I'm still in the house and I'm sweating just trying to do my hair. After three extremely hot summers, I thought my parents would've installed air conditioners by now, but no. And my fan is on its last legs. *Pitiful.* But if I don't hurry, I'm going to be late for practice, and if that happens, my coach can disqualify me from competition. So I put my hundreds of micro-braids into a ponytail. It's better this way 'cause it won't mess me up when I'm jumping. I don't know how my friends can fuss with their hair *and* put on makeup in this heat. They do it just to look cute for the boys, who barely pay attention to them anyway. We're only thirteen; we'll have plenty of time for boys later. Besides, they have no idea how they look after practice. All those makeup shades and mascara mixed with dripping sweat make for one colorful hot mess.

I rush out of my room to find my little brother playing games. Literally. Cameron is sitting on the steps playing on his kiddie tablet with one sock laid out right next to him and the other at the top of the stairs. "Cameron!" He never does what I ask. Then again, he's only seven. "Cameron, did you put socks on your feet before you put on your sneakers?" I can see he didn't. "Cameron!" Having a little brother requires patience, and right now I don't have any.

"Cam, I've got to get out of here. You should have been ready an hour ago, like I asked you." This boy is not even paying attention to me. So I snatch his toy away. "Go get your other sock and come right back down here. Now!"

"Stop yelling at me." Cameron hates me yelling at him as much as I hate my mother yelling at us, but it's just so darn effective. I quickly wrestle the socks onto his feet and tie his sneakers, and we're out the door. *Finally.*

• • •

My mother was supposed to drop Cameron off at the baby-sitter's on her way out, but she said she had to leave early. Said she had something important to do. I am guessing it had something to do with my dad, because she had that serious I'm-about-to-kick-somebody's-butt look on her face. My mother usually acts all dignified, but she's feisty. And when she's suspicious of somebody messing around with him, my mother gets *really* jealous. One time she cursed out a cashier at the supermarket who was flirting with my dad while my mom was standing right next to him. Sometimes I overhear women in my neighborhood talking about how my father is too handsome for his own good and that my mother puts up with too much of his stuff—well, they use other words, but I get their point.

Truthfully, my parents are a soap opera in and of themselves. They should call a TV network and have people follow them around with cameras. They would make one crazy reality show. Especially my father; he doesn't mind the attention, but my mother does. So when they argue and get mad at each other—which is every other week—they almost forget they have kids, and that's how I end up stuck with Cameron. A lot. It seems like ever since Cameron came along, my parents have been fighting more often. I don't think their problems have anything to do with him, but I twist my lips and raise an eyebrow to the possibility that they just might. *We don't look anything alike.* When I was about six years old, my dad left my mom and me for one reason or another, and they were apart for some time. They got back together, then Cameron was born. All I know is that I spend more time with Cameron than they ever do.

And all of this drama is why I got into double Dutch. It's the only time I have to myself, and when I'm between the ropes, I feel free. I'm focused on two things: keep jumping, and don't mess up. I don't let anything get into my head that will make me dwell on what's going on at home. In the ropes, it's about me, about how many perfect jumps I can do in two minutes. So when my parents started tripping, double Dutch became my outlet. That and my diary, which is the only place my secrets are safe. By fifth grade, I was hooked on double Dutch. Now that I just finished seventh grade, I love it, and it still keeps my mind off how unfair my parents can be sometimes. I may be a kid, but I'm not stupid; I know something crazy is going on. I guess I'll find out what the new episode of *The Real House Lives of Sarah & Johnnie* is later tonight. It's probably just another silly fight. At least I hope it is.

The babysitter living so close is cool; walking past the guys at the corner is not. I can't help but notice them beyond the trees, beyond the little kids playing hopscotch on the chalked sidewalk and people sweeping their steps. Summer just started, and they've found absolutely nothing else to do but buzz around in front of the bodega like a bunch of bees waiting to sting anyone who gets in their way. With music blaring from tall speakers on the sidewalk causing all this unnecessary noise, these boys will stand there all day sniffing behind girls, looking for honey. I hate to walk past the swarm, but there's no time to cross the street. Besides, showing fear isn't something you do around here. I just don't have time for saggy-pants-wearing, up-to-no-good boys. And like clockwork, one of them steps in my way.

" 'Ey, girl. Where you going? Can I come?" some random boy asks.

I pay him no mind and walk around him.

"Leave my sister alone!" Cameron yells back.

I yank Cameron closer and drag him as fast as his feet can shuffle. The three boys laugh at my little brother's only defense, which makes me kind of sorry that I yelled at him earlier. The corner boys' constant catcalling and begging is annoying, but I hate to admit that it does boost my ego, even if they aren't my type. They think I'm pretty, I guess. *Am I?* It's hard to tell, since they do that to every girl who passes by. Maybe if one of them pulled their pants up, wore a shirt, and got a real haircut, I might stop to say "What's up?" My mother thinks I'm too picky and that I'll never find a boyfriend if I keep acting so uptight. Who said I was looking for a boyfriend, anyway? A boy is the furthest thing from my mind right now. I have a double Dutch tournament coming up.

Thank goodness Ms. Sharine is waiting for us in front of her brownstone home, or I'd really be late for practice. Once I hand Cameron off, I run the next three blocks to make it to the gym on time!

One Jump Closer

I pull open the rickety doors of the old, run-down community center gym, praying Ms. Jackson doesn't see me sneaking in. She is one short, curvy lady who used to be double Dutch champion in her day, so she doesn't play when it comes to tardiness. Even if I'm five minutes early, I'm considered late. Ugh! She's so hard to please. Good, she's busy directing the junior coaches. *Dang.* It's crowded this year. As soon as the double Dutch league came to Bedford-Stuyvesant, it seemed like every kid who thought they could jump joined quicker than they could post flyers around town. There are even boys here. *What? Really?* Ever since some boys from Japan showed up at the Holiday

Classic at the Apollo—one of my dream competitions—
two years in a row and won the whole thing, suddenly
all the boys in Brooklyn think they can jump too. *Cute,
but whatever.* Girls still rule. Boys . . . hmm, maybe that's
why this graffiti-covered gym is twice as funky as it usually is. Some of these kids need to learn to use deodorant.
For reals.

I don't know if my heart is beating hard out of fear of
Ms. Jackson seeing me or because the sound of the ropes
hitting the floor is inviting me to the National Jump-off
at the end of the summer. It feels like I've waited my
whole life to compete in the nationals—well, since fifth
grade—and now it's finally here. No longer will I compete against girls my age and younger and be known as
"one of the best middle schoolers" in Brooklyn. I finally
have the opportunity to compete with the older kids for
the chance at becoming a junior high national champion.
And that's exactly what I plan to do. Even at practice,
other kids show respect because I'm always wearing my
game face *and* I hold the title for speed. Now I'm here
to win bragging rights for another year and on a whole
new level. So it doesn't matter if we have to jump double
Dutch in a funky cardboard box. I want to make it to the
jump-off.

I see my team—Mimi, Nikki, Drea, and Eva—sitting
on the floor. *What?*

"Why are you guys sitting around? You should be warming up," I say, and mean it. *Seriously, though.*

"We're waiting on you, Kayla. We thought you weren't coming," Mimi retorts after she pulls her thumb out of her mouth. Even though we're on our way to eighth grade, Mimi still sucks her thumb like a kindergartner. It's weird, but she's my best friend and she never backs down from my bossiness.

"When have I ever *not* shown up for practice?" I ask incredulously.

"You're captain of the team. You're never supposed to be late either," Mimi answers back, and stands up. "So what's the problem?"

"I had to take care of my little brother. My mother . . . Look, can we just get to jumping?" I don't have time to put my family's business in the street, nor do I want to. I just grab the ropes and begin untangling them.

No one says another word. We all just assume our positions. Mimi and Eva turn while Drea and I jump. Drea is a little chubby, probably from eating a lot of her *abuela*'s rice and beans, but she can jump like nobody's business and she's a really good turner. Eva is a lot like me, and sometimes we bump heads on ideas, but after a few frustrating arguments we've realized we make each other better. And although Eva's glasses make her look nerdy, she's quite bossy herself. Sometimes she gives me this feeling like she's jealous of me or something. But whatever; they're my friends, and we make a great team. And because we've known each other since third grade, unfortunately they know things aren't always cool at my house. So I just push whatever is going on at home to the back of my mind and focus on the ropes. We get started with the warm-up routine that we all know inside out. Two of us turn, two jump, then we switch as we sing our warm-up song.

Jump in! Jump in! Warm those legs till they burn!
Get loose! Get loose! Watch the ropes while
   they turn.
Pick up your feet, pick up the pace! No time for
   us to waste.
Keep up! Keep up! No time-out.
Let's show 'em what the Double Dutch Jets are
   all about!
Go! Go! Go! Go! Go!

We're moving so fast that everybody stops and stares. We take up as much space as we need to do our tricks: cartwheels in and out of the ropes, double high hops, knee lifts, twirls, and other stuff we do carefully so we don't catch the ropes with our feet. Everyone clears away, giving us room 'cause we're just too fly for a small area.

We get to my favorite part: speed. I always try to beat my last time and jumps per minute. *Whistle!* Ms. Jackson calls it quits on warm-ups. Even after the whistle, I still speed-jump.

"Keep turning!" I demand.

"One-two, one-two," Mimi says to keep me on track.

Eva rolls her eyes but turns feverishly while Drea thumbs the clicker on a handheld counter. After a few more speedy jumps, my feet catch the ropes. I haven't even broken a sweat. *Whistle!*

"What's the count?" I ask in a big breath.

"Three hundred seventeen," Drea answers with a smile.

Any number over three hundred jumps within two minutes is very impressive to judges. But before we can get excited about our progress, Ms. Jackson blows her whistle for the third time.

"I'm not going to blow this whistle again! I need y'all to come front and center!" Ms. Jackson yells as she pops gum. My mom says popping gum is tacky, but Ms. Jackson has mastered it like a form of art. She says it helps her dieting, and she's probably on a new one now 'cause she's killing that gum. Either way, Ms. Jackson is always blaming her crankiness on her diet and telling us that "you need not get on my nerves." *Whoops.* I think I already did.

Having been one of the famous Double Dutch Divas,

Ms. Jackson is familiar with the addiction to double Dutch, but she will not be disrespected by any "wannabe" champions, as she says so often. She's constantly telling us how she struggles to volunteer her time and loves seeing us having fun, and how she believes someday we'll keep the dream alive of bringing double Dutch to newer heights, maybe even making it an Olympic sport. In the meantime, she'll "be damned if you all drive me crazy." Ms. Jackson clutches her clipboard in one hand and rests the other on her hip. Her gum-smacking slows down as she stares at my team, the Double Dutch Jets, but mainly me, as we find a spot on the gym floor.

"Double Dutch is not just about jumping rope. It's also about respecting the sport, fellow jumpers, and everyone involved. And I don't have to explain the meaning of 're-spect' to you again, do I?" Ms. Jackson says, expecting the right answer.

"No, Ms. Jackson," the group says in unison.

"Good, 'cause when I blow this whistle, that means it's time to stop what you're doing and listen up." Ms. Jackson says this looking dead at me, and then at the rest of the Jets. "Do I make myself clear?"

"Yes, Ms. Jackson," we all answer respectfully.

I know Ms. Jackson is referring to me. I twist my lips and roll my eyes, which I know she hates, but I can't help it. Some of the kids are here just for fun, but I'm here to compete and win *big*. I think she understands my mission more than she cares to let me know, so she just gets on with her business.

"Now, I've got some good news and some bad news. The good news is, regionals leading up to the National Jump-off at Madison Square Garden will start next week," Ms. Jackson informs us. Everybody gets all excited. "Wait a minute, now. Let me finish." She tries to settle us down. "The bad news is that not everyone from this league will make the cut," she says matter-of-factly. The crowd moans.

"I don't know about you guys, but I'm going to be in that competition," I say without hesitation. There is a murmur among the teams about who's going and who's not. Some of them don't think I can hear whispering that we're—well, that *I'm*—conceited and stuck-up. *Whatever.* My team is good and they know it.

"All right, everyone, settle down. And, Ms. MaKayla Mac, if you don't humble yourself, you and the rest of the Double Dutch Jets won't be going anywhere," Ms. Jackson replies with attitude. *No, she didn't just call me by my full name.* The *ooooh*s swell in the room like I'm supposed to be embarrassed.

"That goes for all of you," Ms. Jackson continues.

I wave off the comment, but then I suddenly realize, *If she called me out, then that means we made the cut!* I quickly jump to my feet. "Does this mean my team is in?"

Ms. Jackson hesitates a moment because she didn't intend to start the announcements that way, but she knows she let the cat out of the bag. "Yes! You guys are going to the regionals," she confirms.

We all go crazy! Ms. Jackson knows she has to continue announcing the competing teams or jealousy might get out of hand. So she runs off the team names. "Triple Double Trouble! The Loosey Gooseys! Jumping Jacks!" Ms. Jackson yells over the crowd, and several more teams scream as the gym continues to erupt. As she finishes with the list, Ms. Jackson looks over her clipboard to find a few sad faces. She doesn't look too closely or else she might get emotional herself, since she knows how badly all the jumpers want a shot at the big dance. Lastly, she announces that parents are welcome at the competition. Maybe both my parents will come for once, since it will be my first real competition. I quickly throw the idea right out of my mind because I know my parents will find some excuse why they can't make it. *Kayla, honey, not today. I'm so tired and I have so much to do. Maybe next time,* my mother will say, and my father, well, if the sport doesn't involve a ball, then it must not be serious. But double Dutch is serious to me. It's the only thing that keeps me sane. Then, suddenly Ms. Jackson is in my face.

"Remember what I said, Ms. Kayla. Don't let that little ego of yours get in the way of your success. Being good and proud is one thing, but arrogance will only invite enemies and distractions," she says, sealing her speech with a piercing look, as if she can see my soul.

"Why are you always chastising me? You ain't my mother," I tell her.

"And you're so lucky I'm not. Now, I know your mother, and I know she didn't raise a disrespectful, rude child," she says sternly, but I stand defiant. Did she really have to go there in front of my friends? I am not a child, and she shouldn't be talking to me that way. The only reason I keep my mouth shut is because I don't want to mess up our chances of making it to the Garden.

"Are you finished?" I ask. Ms. Jackson is on my last nerve now, and I'm on hers.

"No," Ms. Jackson continues. "As your coach, it is my duty to tell you that I think you have great potential and that I can see you going far in this sport or anything you set your mind to. But if you don't check that rough-and-tough attitude of yours, you'll never see what I'm talking about."

I still stand there with my arms crossed, staring at her

as if to say, *Can I go now?* My friends walk off and act like they weren't listening, but I know they heard Ms. Jackson checking me. Finally she moves out of my way, and I catch up with my team. Ms. Jackson doesn't really know me, so . . . *whatever!* She can't tell me how to act. I'm my own boss. My team made it to the regionals for the National Jump-off, our first real tournament. Nothing can stop us now!

Reality Bites

After practice, it's still hot out and we're so hungry. We've been jumping for three hours straight, we made up a whole new routine, and we need something to eat—and fast. Normally we'd go to the pizza shop, but it's a few blocks away. So we make a quick stop at the bodega, aka the corner store hangout. The storefront is oddly visible, since the boys who are usually standing there are gone. *Probably out doing bad boy stuff.* I know that not all the boys in Brooklyn are bad, but the ones hanging out around the stores usually have nothing else to do except get into trouble. As we devour our snacks on the way home, the Jets can't stop talking about the big news. We've all heard rumors about the competition at Madison Square Garden, but none of us have ever been.

"I heard the Southern teams are incredible," Drea says in an intimidated voice.

"They jump double Dutch in the South?" I ask. "What do they know about jumping double Dutch?" I mean, *really*.

"What? Are you kidding? Almost every state in the nation—every country on the planet—has a team," Mimi interjects. "I thought you knew that."

"Even Japan and Denmark. Denmark! Come on!" Eva adds.

"I knew about the foreign countries, but the South?" I question.

"I heard the coaches talking about some of them, and they said the Southern teams are really good," Drea adds.

"So what? That doesn't mean they can beat us. We're the best in the world, right?" I ask, hoping for agreement but hearing only soft *yeah*s. "We'll just have to practice hard. I'll see you guys tomorrow. *On time,* I promise," I say as we reach my front steps.

Before anybody says another word, we hear a commotion coming from inside my brownstone. I look at my friends, who share a knowing look. *Oh my gosh, not again!* It's my parents. They're yelling like they want the whole neighborhood to hear them. They're so embarrassing! My friends give the peace sign and quickly say their good-byes. I think I even hear Eva say, "Good luck with that." *Ugh!* Why do my parents have to be so loud? I run up the stairs past Cameron, who is very much into his tablet.

"What are they fighting about now?" I ask, frustrated.

"Daddy just got home . . . since yesterday morning," says Cameron, barely distracted from his game.

Being the big sister and now a referee, I push through the heavy wooden doors and practically race down the hall to the kitchen, where it seems like round twelve of a yelling match is taking place. Before I can say a word, my mother fumbles to her bedroom and starts throwing stuff into the hallway. It's my dad's stuff. Maybe today is the last straw for whatever he did. I don't think my dad's good looks are going to save him this time. Today something is really wrong.

I want to jump in, but I'm too afraid. They're so angry. My mother's face is a beautiful mess of tears and makeup. Even as she fusses with my father, her husband of thirteen years, anyone can see how much she still loves him, and my dad has always been proud to have a beautiful woman like my mother; I think it's what keeps him putting up with their tumultuous relationship. Maybe everyone in the neighborhood is right about my father. Maybe he is a "ladies' man" who can't seem to keep his hand out of the cookie jar; in other words, people think he's a player. I hope the rumors aren't true, but I'm no fool. There are a lot of single mothers around my neighborhood who would love to have my father as their man.

Instantly my eyes begin to well with tears. When my mother cries, I cry too.

"You want to stay out all night?" my mom asks through her rage. "Then take your clothes with you and get out!"

"I told you, I was working!" my father yells back.

"Right! Work! How many times are you going to use that excuse?" My mom continues to throw stuff from the closet. "I'm tired of it, Johnnie! And you can tell 'work' she can have you!"

"Sarah!" my dad pleads.

"Get out!" my mom yells at the top of her lungs.

"Stop! Stop! Please, stop it!" I yell at them, as if they are the kids now. Miraculously they stop. My mother plops onto the bed, sobbing.

"You're impossible to deal with!" my dad screams.

"Daddy, please stop!" I say with as much respect as I can muster up.

After calming himself with a few deep breaths, my dad realizes the mess they've made. He quickly gathers whatever shirts and pants he can and practically levitates with anger. He heads for the door at full steam. He passes Cameron on the way out, barely noticing him.

"Bye, Daddy." Cameron looks up from his game with sadness in his eyes.

"Son, we'll catch up later, all right?" Daddy says, trying to conceal his own disappointment. Cameron doesn't make a move. Sadly, my little brother seems to have lost confidence in my father at that moment, and he concentrates harder on his game. After Daddy lets out a big sigh, he runs out to his shiny car. I go to the living room window and watch him drive away. I can't help but wonder where he's going. Tears fall and disappear in the sweat on my T-shirt from double Dutch. I cover my face as I run to my room. I don't want Cameron to see me cry. He doesn't need to see *everyone* falling apart. Just like me, Cameron is probably wondering: *Will Daddy be back?*

Change Is Gonna Come

It's the first day of regionals on the way to the National Jump-off, and some kids are milling about nervously as if it's Judgment Day. Well, it is, but some aren't too confident about their double Dutch skills, unlike me. Even though I've been dealing with the drama at home for a week, I still believe my team is ready. I just push my issues at home to the back of my mind and arrive early to jump about a thousand times with a single rope. But no matter what I do, no matter how much I try to forget what's going on, I constantly think of my mom and dad. I wonder how two people who supposedly love each other can fight so much. When things were good, they'd hug and kiss all the time. Now I just don't understand. Maybe I'm too young to understand. If this is what marriage is about, I don't think I'll ever get married. For now I have to get focused. *With all this anger and sadness, I am so ready to smash any competition!*

"Hey, Kayla, is your mom coming? Maybe my mom can sit with yours?" Nikki breaks my concentration.

"Oh, um, my mom . . . couldn't make it," I lie. "But it's only the local competition, right? So, you know, she'll make the next one." This is not the place or time to air my family's dirty laundry, although I'm sure everyone's already smelled it. Nikki suspects grief, but thankfully she doesn't pry. When my parents fight, they completely forget about me and Cameron. So asking them to take time out of their busy day to show up to my silly double Dutch competition would be like trying to take a toy from a baby. They'd just whine about it.

Whistles sound all around, and thank goodness the competition gets everyone in game-time mode. There are mostly girls, ages six to fourteen, jumping carefully in the compulsory test. In compulsory, teams have to show they can make two turns to the right on the right foot and two turns to the left on the left foot, do two crisscross jumps, both with each foot crossing over once, then ten high steps, and exit the ropes, all without making a mistake. It sounds complicated, but it's easy-peasy, especially since everyone does it slowly and carefully so they don't mess up. The Double Dutch Jets sail smoothly through compulsory. Speed is up next—my favorite. Other kids stop to stare at me. I think I'm maybe one of the—if not *the*—fastest speed jumper they've ever seen. Not bragging either. I'm just saying.

Before entering the ropes I keep my head down. My concentration is on the ropes and only the ropes. As they spin close to my chin, I glance at my teammates as if to say, *You guys know what to do. Let's go!* In less than a second, my feet float between the ropes and I find my groove. I hope the quick pitter-patter of my feet isn't too fast for the judges to count every time my left foot hits the floor for the points. The ropes seem to disappear as they move in a circular motion. I know Drea's and Eva's arms are tightening up by now, but my girls are making it happen. As I look down at my clean white sneakers, they appear to flicker like a flame.

"Come on, Kayla! One-two, one-two!" Drea cheers. No one has any idea that I am imagining that all my parents' issues are under my feet. The problem is, I don't even know what their issues are. I have my suspicions, though. Tap-tap-tap-tap-tap-tap-tap! *My feet are on fire!* The faster I jump, the better I feel.

Time! Two minutes felt like two seconds. I exit the ropes as easily as I went in. "Three hundred and thirty-two steps," the judge calls to the panel. It's a new novice record! My teammates and I celebrate.

"If we don't get to the finals with that number, those judges are crazy!" Mimi says reassuringly.

"I counted three hundred twenty-nine," Eva adds. "But whatever they say counts, right?" I grimace at her a bit with my hands on my hips. *Did she really just say that?*

"That's right," Drea says in a huff. "We're in!"

A smile shows up on my face for the first time this morning, but it doesn't last, since neither of my parents is here to see me. Even Ms. Jackson has sort of a grin on her face while still popping her gum.

"That's how you do it, girl. Keep your eye on the prize, no matter what's going on around you," Ms. Jackson says. What does she mean by that? *Does she know something I don't?* But before I can catch my breath to ask, Ms. Jackson moves on.

After the competition, I quickly grab my stuff and run home as fast as I can to tell my parents the good news. Maybe it'll change their moods and make them forget what they've been fighting about. I can only wish. I enter my house, and the door hits something behind it. *Why are there suitcases in the hall?* I don't see or hear anybody. *What is going on?*

"Ma? Anybody home?" I call.

Finally I find my mother in the kitchen having a cup of coffee. She doesn't seem very happy, but maybe I can cheer her up.

"Ma, guess what—I made it to the next round!" I say, beaming with excitement, hoping she'll at least smile. Nothing. "I mean, me and the rest of the Double Dutch Jets, but you know." I grab the orange juice out of the refrigerator. "I'm the one who put us on the map." I'm joking, but Mom still isn't laughing with me.

"That's nice, baby," she says, withdrawn. "I'm going to need a favor from you and your brother, okay?"

"Sure. What's up with the luggage in the front? I mean, I don't know what's going on with you and Daddy, but . . ." I pour myself some juice, trying not to panic.

"I need you and Cameron to spend the rest of the summer with Aunt Jeanie," my mom blurts out, cutting me off.

"No! Aunt Jeanie? In North Carolina? Ma, I hate that place! I just told you I made it into the next round in the double—"

"MaKayla!" my mom says as she stands quickly. "I don't need this right now, okay? Just go! Go to your room and pack your things."

"But, Ma, I have a chance to make it to Madison Square

26

Garden! I can't leave now! Ma, you gotta . . ." Tears quickly flood my eyes.

"Your father and I are talking about divorce!" she yells over me. I'm suddenly breathless. "Now, I didn't want to tell you that, but it's . . . Things are not good right now. I am sorry." Her voice quivers. She sits quietly. Although I want to fight to stay, I don't want to make my mother feel any worse than she already does.

"This isn't fair!" I cry uncontrollably, and stomp all the way to my room like a five-year-old. I can't help it. How could this be happening? *I've worked so hard!* Cameron opens his door, only to shake his head at me. What does he care? He's a kid.

Southbound

When morning comes, I can barely open my eyes. They're swollen shut from crying so much, and getting out of bed is like pulling teeth. I just don't want to do it. Unfortunately I don't think staying in bed is going to change my mother's horrible decision to send us down south. She doesn't care that I hate everything about it. It's like time stands still there, and it's so darn quiet! And to top it off, my cousin Sally and I may be the same age, but we just don't get along. *Ugh!* My parents are fighting, and Cameron and I are the ones who have to pay by having our lives turned upside down.

I stuff my last pair of sneakers into my bag and head downstairs to wait for my dad. *Wait!* My double Dutch ropes! I stop to think. If I take them with me, they will probably sit in some corner collecting old country dust, since I've never seen *anyone* playing double Dutch there. I mean, my cousin used to, but my mom tells me she's a ballerina now. *Figures.* Bringing my ropes would only remind me of what I'd be missing back here in Brooklyn. So I just grab my diary off the dresser and sadly leave my ropes behind. At least I'll have plenty of time to catch up on my entries. As for my double Dutch dreams, they're done.

Mimi and Eva come by to see me off, but I think there's more to it than that.

"I'm so sorry you have to leave." Mimi hugs me.

"I think it's going to be fun." Eva joins in the hug. "If I was leaving Brooklyn for the summer, I'd be ecstatic!"

"That's because you've never been to North Carolina. You guys don't understand. My cousin is a snooty little princess, and I hate being someplace where I don't know anyone." I can't help how I feel. The South just sucks to me. I'm a city girl, born and bred, and that's how I'll stay for the rest of my life.

"I'm sure you'll make new friends. Maybe even meet a boy," Mimi says as she nudges me with a smile. I know she's trying to cheer me up, but I just give her a crazy look and continue to pout. *Really?* Like a boy is better than jumping double Dutch.

"Well, uh, since you're going to be gone, uh, we're going to have to replace you," Eva says hesitantly, then, "Oooh, I think I know someone!" I look at her like, *I haven't left yet. I'm still standing here. Hello?*

"Whatever. I guess you gotta do what you gotta do," I say as they stare at each other. "I mean, yeah, you should. Make sure you find somebody good. Even though I'll be gone, I am still a Jet."

"Of course you are," agrees Mimi. "It won't be the same without you."

"Yeah, she won't be here to boss us around all summer," Eva mutters under her breath. Mimi shoots her a look. "What? I'm just agreeing with you," Eva says, cleaning up her comment. "I mean, who's going to push us to make it past the semifinals?"

"No worries. You guys can make it without me," I say truthfully. "It's our—well, *your*—big chance. If I were you, I wouldn't blow it either."

"We won't," Mimi responds.

I somehow get the feeling Eva is honestly happy I'll be away for the summer. She probably hates me for making her turn all the time, but the other girls are just better jumpers than she is. There's nothing I can do about that.

As captain of the team, I have to call the shots how I see fit. I just try not to dwell on the negative and instead "accentuate the positive," as they tell us at school. Or maybe Eva *is* really glad she won't have to deal with me bossing everyone around. I can admit, I'm bossy at times. *That's just me.* And my *real* friends accept me that way. It's probably my bossiness that got us closer to the competition at Madison Square Garden anyway, and if they make it without me, I'll be happy for them. They're my girls and I'm going to miss them, including Eva.

My father finally pulls up in front of the house. Cameron drags his last bag to the top of the steps while my mother straightens the jacket she put on him, which he quickly takes off. It's like a hundred degrees in the shade! My father waves at my mom from the car, but she just ignores him. One thing I won't miss is all the tension and loud, embarrassing arguments between them.

"It might be cold on the plane, so keep your jacket handy, sweetie." My mother babies my brother, which he soaks up until he sees my friends.

"Okay, Ma." Cameron makes his way down the stairs to my dad, who's standing outside the car, waiting.

"Well, I guess I'll see you guys when I get back," I tell Mimi and Eva as I grab my bags. My dad comes over to help me.

"You all act like it's the end of the world," my father says, attempting to make a joke.

"It might as well be," I say as I turn to my friends. "Make it to the Garden. No matter what, you guys better bring it."

"We got you, Kayla," Mimi says unconvincingly. The three of us have another group hug. My mother is suddenly by my side. She looks at my sad face, then kisses me on the cheek.

"Here." Mom hands me a picture of my North Carolina relatives.

"Ma, I know what they look like," I say, annoyed that she thinks I have forgotten them. *I could never forget them.*

"I am just making sure, sweetie," my mom says. She hesitates, then adds, "I can't promise you that everything will be the same when you get back, but I need to count on you to be strong, okay?"

I just nod somberly. My parents possibly splitting up isn't something I want to think about. *What will happen to us? Will my father leave us? Will we have to choose sides? Will my little brother and I be split apart?* And now I won't even have double Dutch to take my mind off the situation.

"Have Aunt Jeanie call me when you get there," my mom orders. I nod again.

My father takes the bag out of my hand with a smile. "Hey, baby girl," he says.

By the look I give him he should know I'm not happy with him right now. *Can't he tell?* I know I'm being punished for something he did. He stares at my mother for a few seconds, but she looks away. "Hop in, Kayla. GPS says we're looking at traffic." My father hurries me along. As he shuts the front passenger door, I wave to Mimi and Eva, who start walking down the block. Eva smiles a bit, which makes me feel like she's definitely not sad about me leaving. My mother solemnly waves from the top of the stairs, hiding her tears.

Within minutes there's an awkward silence in the car. Even Cameron is quiet. Maybe because my mother packed his tablet. My father starts trying to make small talk about the weather and how much hotter it's going to get, stuff I couldn't care less about right now. *Really, Dad?* I pull out my earbuds, stuff them into my ears as far as they can go, and crank up the volume on my tablet to deafen the angry voices in my head. My father's moving his mouth, but I can't hear a word he's saying. *Thank goodness!* Suddenly he yanks the cord.

"I'm talking to you," my father says.

"Come on, Daddy!" I say, aggravated. "What's wrong with you?"

"That tone is unacceptable, so I suggest you find a new one." Now *he's* agitated. "I would like to have a conversation with you if you don't mind," he presses.

"Do you have a girlfriend?" He wants to talk, right? *So let's get down to it.*

"What?" He's caught off guard. "That is none of your business. And frankly that isn't what I want to talk about."

"I do," I persist. "It *is* our business, because Cameron and I have to go down south because you and Mommy are fighting, and it had nothing to do with us, but we're the ones paying for whatever mistake you made."

"You know, you've become very opinionated and outspoken lately, young lady, and I'm not sure I like it." My dad is trying to change course here, but he can tell by my crossed arms and raised eyebrows that I am very serious about hearing an answer.

"Daddy, I'm not a kid anymore," I try to reason. "I know when something is going on."

"So do you have a girlfriend?" Cameron asks.

Shocked, my father checks his rearview mirror and realizes Cameron is in on the conversation. He glances back at me, and I give him the same look I did earlier. *Well?* Daddy sighs as he searches for words.

"Your mother and I haven't been getting along for some time now. But you know"—he looks away for a moment—"she's just very hard to live with."

"And you're easy to live with? Hmm," I mumble. *Is he for real?*

"What was that?" Dad asks.

I shrug and look out the window.

"You leave your socks everywhere, and Mommy makes me pick them up," Cameron chimes in.

I snicker. Daddy shoots me a look.

"Okay, maybe not," he admits. "But the story is a lot deeper than that. I mean, your mother and I were so young when we got married. We hardly knew each other. . . . Look, I want you both to know that no matter what we decide, we will make sure we don't miss a beat with you, and we'll be there for you one hundred percent."

"So you really are thinking about getting a divorce?" I ask with sadness. Daddy doesn't respond.

"What's a divorce?" Cameron is so innocent. "Is that code for 'we're getting a dog'?"

"No, Cameron." I try to cover. "It's when two people play Ping-Pong with their kids and think it's better that way."

"I like Ping-Pong." Cameron doesn't get it.

"I like Ping-Pong too, buddy," Dad responds. "But don't get too excited. We might not be playing for a while. Just hang tight, okay?"

"Do you still love Mommy?" I ask.

"Of course I do," he says as he squints and gives me the side-eye. To that I raise an eyebrow at him, as if to ask, *Love-love or just love?*

Daddy starts to speak, then hesitates. It's like he wants to say something but doesn't know how to tell us the truth. He just lets out a big sigh and focuses on the road. And I go back to listening to my music. *Ugh!* Love seems so complicated, which is exactly why I can't even *think* about having a boyfriend. If love comes with this many headaches, I'd rather not even go there, ever!

When we arrive at the airport, the tension in the car is still suffocating; I can't wait to get out. Now even the lady at the ticket counter is flirting with my dad. *Can't she see he has kids?* Flirting back comes easy to my dad. It's like it's in his DNA. They laugh and joke throughout the whole process of shipping us away.

"Hold on to these." Dad hands me the tickets. "Make sure you call when you land. You hear me?"

"Call you with what?" I ask. "I never did get that phone you promised when I got to junior high."

"If you keep talking to me with that attitude, you'll never get one," Dad responds. "Is that clear?"

"Yes, Daddy." I nod, with sadness and frustration written on my face. My father grabs my shoulders.

"Listen, your mother and I have some things to work out, and nothing is certain," he says.

"Why not?" I ask, really not understanding.

"Because life is about constantly making the best decisions." *Is Dad trying to be philosophical?* "You know, life doesn't come with instructions, and neither does marriage. Just know that your mother and I love you both very much." He pulls out a wad of money and peels off a few bills. "Here, I think you guys can have a good time with this."

"This is supposed to make us happy?" I say, angry and disappointed. "A few hundred dollars?"

"I'll take it!" Cameron says happily as I hold him back.

"Kayla, I told you, you need to check that tone of yours." My dad's patience wanes. "I am still your father."

"Then act like it!" I grab the money and Cameron's arm and move quickly toward the escalator. I can't help it. I'm going to suffer my whole summer because "life is about constantly making the best decisions." *Whatever!* I am going to miss my friends, the double Dutch competition, and everything about being home for the summer. This *sucks*!

Daddy watches as we go up the escalator. He looks upset, but he knows he only has himself to blame. Maybe I am being hard on him because I don't know what's really going on. My mother might be a witch when Cameron and I aren't around, for all I know. But regardless of what my dad says now, he's always taught me that when I start something I should finish it; never leave unfinished business. He's not practicing what he preaches. Hopefully he won't leave *us* unfinished.

37

On the plane, Cameron and I settle next to a little old lady. Tears stream down my face as I watch the New York City skyline fade away in the clouds. I feel a tap on my hand. It's the lady, holding out a tissue.

"Are you all going home or will you be visiting in Charlotte?" she asks with a friendly smile.

"We're going to visit relatives," I reply as I wipe my face.

"Oh, well then, why such a long face?" she asks. "Charlotte is wonderful in the summertime. I think you're really going to enjoy it, maybe even have the best time of your life."

This lady has obviously never met my cousin Sally. If she had, she wouldn't assume it's going to be fun hanging out with her. I crack a smile to be polite. At this point, all I can do is close my eyes and dream of being back in Brooklyn, but all the hope in the world isn't stopping my tears. The best time of my life? *I seriously doubt it.*

North Carolina State of Mind

I jump out of a deep sleep, hoping all of this is a bad dream. But, no, the plane just made a hard landing in blue-skied North Carolina. I can't believe we're here already! I probably dozed off while the little old lady was still talking to me. Where is she? She must have changed her seat. I look around the rows, but I still don't see her. Maybe she was a ghost? Maybe she was some kind of fairy godmother telling me I just might have the best time of my life. *Ha!* I can only wish. Cameron slept the whole way too, and now I have to practically drag him off the plane.

At baggage claim, I look around for familiar faces, but I don't see anyone. Until I hear a voice that sounds like my mother's. It's my aunt Jeanie.

"Well, hello there, lady!" Aunt Jeanie says, ever cheerful. She hugs Cameron first. "Look at you! So big! And, Ms. Kayla, my, how you've grown into a beautiful young lady. You're looking more and more like your mother." *Really?* I don't think I have half the beauty of my mother. "Hi, Aunt Jeanie." I smile, still groggy from the plane ride. I forgot how nice she is.

Aunt Jeanie and my mom are like night and day but equally pretty. She's tall and always so put together, and for some crazy reason she always has a smile on her face. I admire her happiness. *Okay, I admit, it really is good to see Aunt Jeanie.* Then, out of the corner of my eye, I see the rest of my relatives. As they approach, Sally stares me up and down. I return the grit and the same tired wave she gives me. She's still short. Still wears her hair in a bun. A bun-head ballerina, I'm guessing. Okay, she's gotten prettier. *Whatever. I still can't stand her.* The last time I was here we didn't get along, not even for a minute. When she wanted to play with dolls, I wanted to climb trees. When I wanted to play hide-and-seek, she wanted to play on the swings. When I wanted to build a clubhouse out of cardboard boxes, she said she didn't play games that made her look homeless. *Huh? Whatever.* But when I did convince her to play in my uncle's old car and act like we were driving, she pulled a lever around the steering wheel and the car rolled right out into the street with us screaming inside it. We smashed into the neighbor's rose garden, which scratched the paint on my uncle's classic car. I thought his head was going to pop off his shoulders, he was so mad. Sally took the blame for everything, while I went back home. She's hated me ever since.

After grimacing at my hat-to-the-back and all my Brooklyn style that she has none of, Sally just walks ahead with her arms crossed as if she hates that I'm here. *If I could catch the next thing smoking back to JFK, I would.*

My uncle Larry says quick hellos and loads our bags onto a cart. Uncle Larry is quiet at times, but he seems happy that way, and he's the only uncle who doesn't treat me like a child. He has a way of treating everyone like they have some sense about everything, like he does, and he expects everyone to be smart or at least act like they are. Maybe that's why he's a successful businessman.

Cameron is ecstatic to see my younger cousins, Michael and Eddie. Michael is only one year older than Eddie, but he looks like he's growing bigger and way faster than little Eddie. To Cameron, it doesn't matter that they are about two and three years older than him. They take him in like they've known each other since diapers. *Boys.* I'm sure at some point the three are going to get on my nerves, but since our parents haven't paid much attention to Cameron lately, it'll be good for him to forget what's going on back at home. At least he'll have a good time. As for me . . . hmm, I don't know.

"It's going to be an interesting summer," Uncle Larry blurts out to Aunt Jeanie.

"It's going to be a perfect summer." Aunt Jeanie smiles sternly. I'm glad somebody's optimistic.

It's dark by the time we pull up to their house, but I can tell it still looks like something out of a magazine. It's large and white, with a green lawn and flowers for days. All the houses in the area are just as pretty. I feel like we've driven up to a neighborhood out of some movie about the burbs. Just as we arrive, the lights come on, making the house look like a majestic castle. And of course, my cousin Sally is the princess. The only thing that's missing is a gate, but I guess crime isn't an issue here, like it is back in Brooklyn.

I can't remember the last time I walked on or even touched grass, and freshly cut green grass at that. It smells that way, anyway. And as I step out of the air-conditioned car, all of this green stuff makes the humidity feel like cool mist on my skin. My aunt and uncle's house looks like it cost millions, outside and in. There are family pictures everywhere. They've taken a lot of trips. *Lucky them.* The whole house reminds me of the homes my dad used to work on in the Hamptons when I was small. I used to pretend they were my real-life Barbie Dreamhouses and act like I owned the place when I was in one. Only when no one was looking, though. But even here, I'm cautious not to touch Aunt Jeanie's antiques, which I'm sure are just as priceless. The way my mom puts it, Aunt Jeanie has a thing for finding junk and selling it. I think if anyone can make money from selling old stuff, that's pretty cool.

The boys run straight into the huge kitchen and immediately grab snacks out of the cabinet. Cameron is right behind Michael and Eddie as they continue running into their room. He's having fun already. Sally, however, has been completely ignoring me all the way from the airport, so I can't imagine she'll invite me to her room. And I'm right. She goes up the stairs to her bedroom and shuts the door. Aunt Jeanie looks at me and tries to cover for her daughter being inhospitable.

"Sally is . . ." She searches for the right words, then says, "Oh, all right, she's finally become a woman, and she's going through a few things right now."

"Aunt Jeanie!" I wasn't ready for all of that. "I know she doesn't like me. You don't have to make excuses."

"I'm not kidding. She thought it was taking a long time,

and she was beginning to worry," Aunt Jeanie goes on, as if I really want to hear about Sally getting her period. "I think it's all the ballet. But she is very excited to be a woman now."

She notices my uninterested face. "I'm sorry, honey. You must be hungry and exhausted. Here, let Uncle take your stuff upstairs, and I'll warm up something for you."

"I'm fine, really." I begin to think Aunt Jeanie has been wanting someone to talk to and now I'm it.

"Okay, but I made pie," Aunt Jeanie teases.

She finally gets a smile out of me.

"Apple?" I ask as I take a seat in the breakfast nook. Suddenly I feel hunger pangs. Aunt Jeanie's apple pie is *crazy* good. Now, *that* I remember.

Finally, after two servings of pie and ice cream, I am mad sleepy. Aunt Jeanie burns up my ears about my parents and how they met and all. It seems like she is trying to tell me something important, maybe something I need to understand as to why my parents' relationship is so whack right now, but I just can't keep my eyes open. Aunt Jeanie realizes my head has gotten too heavy for my shoulders, because it almost falls into the puddle of melted ice cream on my plate.

"Oh my gosh." Aunt Jeanie jumps, then I jump. "Come on, baby. I just talked you to sleep."

"Huh?" I sit up. She clears our plates and grabs my

arm to help me slide out of the breakfast nook and up the stairs.

"Since Marc is doing an engineering program this summer, he's staying at the dorms in Chapel Hill. You can have his room," Aunt Jeanie says, trying to make up for Sally not sharing her room.

The room is a true boy's room: dark blue paint, basketball hoop on the door, and Beyoncé and JLo posters all over the walls. *Oh boy.* It doesn't matter. I already knew this trip was going to be like living in h-e-double-hockey-sticks, so I am not surprised. And there's an old phone mounted on the wall. *Really?* I always thought Southern people were behind the times, but that's just plain funny. Finally I settle into bed. Not bad. Aunt Jeanie tucks me in like I'm a five-year-old, but it's kind of nice. I've always loved my aunt. She always seems so happy and nice. Wait a minute. . . .

"Aunt Jeanie?" I call. "Is it always this quiet? It's hard to sleep when it's this quiet."

"You city folk are so funny," Aunt Jeanie says, cracking the window. "How about that?"

I hear weird chirping. "What is that?" I ask, annoyed.

"Crickets," Aunt Jeanie explains. "You know, if you count the number of chirps they make within fifteen seconds and add thirty-seven, you can tell what the temperature is outside."

45

Seriously? My . . . eyelids . . . are . . . heavy.

"Okay, good night, sweetie," Aunt Jeanie says from the door. "Oh, and I have a surprise for you and Sally. See you in the morning."

I'm too tired to possibly imagine what the surprise might be, and those cricket chirps are so annoying. And why are Beyoncé and JLo staring at me? I smash a pillow over my head to shut out the weird noises and those stares.

Ugh! I want to go home!

7

Summer Sass

The next morning I don't want to get out of bed, but the delicious aroma of Aunt Jeanie's pancakes makes me dash in and out of the shower quicker than she can call, "Breakfast!" If I remember correctly, my aunt Jeanie's pancakes can make you want more pancakes, but I'm not seven years old anymore. Her cooking could make my stomach swell, which is not good, especially if I'm not jumping double Dutch. I can't even imagine a summer without double Dutch. *The saddest thought.* As I reach the kitchen, it looks like the boys beat me to it, and my brother is still in his pj's.

"Cameron, did you wash your face and brush your teeth?" I ask, knowing he probably didn't.

"Leave me alone, Kayla. I'm on vacation," Cameron says with a mouthful of pancakes. *Ill.*

"That's right," Aunt Jeanie laughs. "You are on vacation, and as soon as you're done I want you three boys to wash up. Uncle Larry and I have surprises for everyone."

Uncle Larry stands at the entrance of the kitchen sipping coffee.

"Good morning, everyone." He is so formal despite his yard clothes and baseball cap. "Yes, we do have a surprise, and we're going to need everyone's full cooperation."

Uh-oh. The last time I was surprised, I got a trip to the South. I don't think I can handle *another* life-altering surprise. I guess my uncle is waiting for little Princess Sally to join us. Finally, dressed neatly like something out of a J.Crew catalog, she saunters slowly down the stairs, sulking as if someone killed the cat she never had. She sure can hold a grudge. *Whatever. I'm over it.* I've already given in to the fact that this is going to be the worst summer ever. But I'm loving that I'll be eating Aunt Jeanie's cooking while I'm here. Pancakes. *Yum!* These fluffy pillows from heaven are perking up my spirits already. I even wave at Sally as thick maple syrup drips from my next bite. *No, she didn't just roll her eyes.*

"Good morning, sweetie," Aunt Jeanie greets her.

"What's so good about it?" Sally drags her sad face to the refrigerator for water.

"Now, Sally, I hope you're not going to keep it up with this sour attitude of yours," Aunt Jeanie replies. "You're going to spoil our surprise."

"What surprise?" Sally looks like she's already disappointed.

"Well," Uncle Larry jumps in, "we're putting in a pool!"

The boys go bananas. I'm even excited about the news, and I don't know how to swim. Sally tries to appear unaffected.

"That's nice," Sally says, slicing an apple.

"The other good news is, the boys are going to help your dad with the pool, and you and Kayla are going to day camp," Aunt Jeanie says, then sips coffee.

"*Day camp?*" Sally is not happy. "I'm too old for day camp." *Day camp? Really?*

"Honey, I hear they're doing something different this year." Aunt Jeanie is selling us the hype. "It's being called the Charlotte Sports Day Camp. It's about encouraging kids to get moving and playing together. You know, teamwork. I think you're going to like it."

"Sounds like fun, Aunt Jeanie." I'm too old for day camp too, but I can't hurt her feelings. I just think it'll be much better than staying cooped up in this house the whole summer.

"You're welcome, baby," Aunt Jeanie replies. "See, Sally? Kayla is excited."

"That's because she still acts like a kid . . . and dresses like one too," Sally says.

"I am not a kid, okay?" I retort. "You're the one who's acting like an ungrateful brat."

"Who are you calling brat?"

"You, Princess!"

"You're just jealous, Kayla."

"Whoa! Hey!" Uncle Larry whistles uncharacteristically. "You two, settle down. Sally, take a seat." Sally plops down at the table.

"Now, look." Aunt Jeanie sighs. "I don't know about you all, but I'm planning on enjoying the next four weeks of this lovely summer with a pool and all the fun. You, Sally, can sit in your room the whole time and pout all you want. Or you can cancel that bad attitude and get with the program." I guess that's Aunt Jeanie's way of trying to sound cool or hip, as she might say. *Funny.* Sally sulks while I snag an extra helping of pancakes. Sally is not spoiling my appetite. "They let me sign you two up even though we were past registration. *And* I had to pay extra," Aunt Jeanie continues. "You'll be a little late, but I think—"

"All right! I'll go to the camp," Sally says, caving. "But if I don't like it, I'll take the sentence and stay in my room."

Aunt Jeanie and Uncle Larry share an inside look. They've seen this act from her before, I'm guessing. Doesn't matter. She isn't me, and I certainly am not sitting in anybody's room . . . for four weeks . . . in the hot South.

Later, Aunt Jeanie drops Princess Sally and me off at a huge community center campus. It's actually what I imagine a country club would look like. Well, I am in the country, so this must be the club. It makes my community center back in Brooklyn look like an old Cracker Jack box. I mean, there's a fountain out in front of something that looks like a lake beside the main building, and there are huge sports fields surrounding the place. Baseball, soccer—is that a skateboard ramp? Wow! This is cool! I feel like I'm at the summer Olympics. The place is crawling with kids, kids my age—and boys who actually have their pants pulled up *over* their underwear. Okay, I must admit, I am a little excited.

"This is the camp?" I ask, just to make sure.

"Sure is," Aunt Jeanie confirms. "Oh, and look. Kids seem like they *want* to be here." She directs that to Sally, who is still uninterested.

"Thanks, Aunt Jeanie," I say, quickly hopping out of the car.

"You're welcome, Kayla." Aunt Jeanie smiles and lowers the window. "You two stick together. You're family, whether you like it or not." Sally and I share an annoyed look. "And family take care of one another." As soon as the car is out of sight, I run off to check out the place, leaving Sally standing with her arms crossed.

Inside, everyone scatters about, checking flyers posted on the walls and then running over to a registration table. There's a guy with a bullhorn announcing what sports are left for signing up. I check out the lists.

Basketball, soccer, baseball, tennis, skateboarding . . . Really? I continue reading. "No friggin' way!" *Double Dutch!!! What?*

I'm at table seven like a lightning bolt struck my butt. I instantly sign up for double Dutch. *Yeah!* I immediately grab the sheet again and sign Sally's name to the list.

"What are you doing?" Sally steams. "You can't just go running off."

"I'm not your child, and if my math is right, I am five months older than you." She's not going to spoil my mood now. "Look! Double Dutch! They have double Dutch teams! I would have never—"

"I hope you didn't . . ." Sally sees her name. "Why did

you do that? I don't want to be on anyone's double Dutch team." She scratches her name from the list.

"What's wrong with you?" I ask. "I know you know how to jump double Dutch. It's like riding a bike—you never forget."

"It's not that!" Sally is upset. "I'm just not into it anymore!"

Suddenly four girls, three white and one Asian, roll up on us like they own the place. They're wearing their own member jackets that read BOUNCING BELLES.

"Is little Sally Walker signing up for double Dutch?" The group laughs. Sally's light brown skin turns pale, as if she's seen a ghost. She's obviously intimidated.

"Who's asking?" I step in front of Sally to get this girl out of her face. *This girl doesn't know—I'm from Brooklyn, and Brooklyn girls don't let anyone intimidate us.*

"The name is Ivy, and I don't know who you are, but your friend here shouldn't even be thinking about signing up for anything double Dutch," she says with a lot of attitude.

I get in her face. "For your information, Sally is my cousin, and she can do whatever she pleases. If she wants to jump double Dutch, she can."

They all bust up laughing.

"Are you sure about that?" says a blond girl.

"Forget them, Kayla." Sally tries to cover. "Let's just go." She grabs my arm, but I don't budge.

"If you know what's good for you, um . . . ?" Ivy pauses.

"Kayla," I say.

"Yeah, whatever," Ivy disses. This *poison* Ivy girl is lucky I don't want to get in trouble on my first day in Charlotte, because she surely would be my *first* reason. "If she knows what's good for her, she better stay away from any competition against us. She will never win." *I can't believe she just said that!* I just stare her down. "Let's go, girls."

"Yeah, you better," I say, holding back. Once they're gone, Sally jumps in my face.

"Why did you do that?" She's shaking and fuming, with watery eyes. "I knew you were going to start trouble!"

"Looks like the trouble started before I got here," I say defensively. But then I realize something. "Who are they, and why are you letting those white girls bully you?"

"White, black, yellow, brown, none of that matters." Sally tries to school me. "Those girls are the Bouncing Belles, and they used to be my friends, my best friends. Just stay out of my business!" Sally rushes away.

"Ooooh, they're the reason why you didn't want to come to camp," I say. Sally doesn't answer as she disappears out of the gym. Something is definitely wrong, and I'm going to find out what. Nobody pushes me or my princess cousin around.

"Hey, kid, are you guys in or out?" An older lady with a scratchy voice asks as she collects sign-up sheets. I grab the one for double Dutch and sign my name and Sally's again, but this time as a team.

"We're in," I answer confidently as I hand the woman the paper. She looks it over.

"You're going to need two more jumpers to make a double Dutch team, sweetie. I don't make 'em, but those're the rules," says the lady. "Teams shut down end of the day tomorrow. If you don't find a pair, you'll be placed elsewhere. Got it?"

I nod. There's no way I'm going to be at this camp and *not* jump double Dutch. Little Sally Walker is going to stand up to those Bouncing *Bullies* if it's the last thing she does this summer. I am going to see to it.

Color-Blind

Since Sally and I are a week late to camp, we've missed tons of "getting to know you" games and have to spend the rest of the day in a crash orientation and tour to learn the rules and regulations, safety measures, blah, blah, blah, but I can't seem to stop smiling. I'm going to be jumping double Dutch again! Wait until I tell my girls back home. *They are going to flip.* Sally, on the other hand, doesn't speak to me the whole time after our run-in with the Bouncing Belles. When my uncle Larry comes to pick us up, he asks how our day was, and Sally immediately tells him that I am starting trouble. We argue all the way through the doors of the house, but once we're inside, Sally runs up to her room and slams the door.

"What is wrong with Sally?" Aunt Jeanie asks, concerned. I shrug out of frustration. Honestly, I don't even know where to begin—her attitude, the fact that she's a party pooper, those bullies—it's all a total mess.

"Something about her old buddies, but I tell you what," Uncle Larry says as he tosses his keys into a basket in the foyer. "She keeps slamming them doors, she can kiss that pool good-bye." He moves away to the backyard as if he knows what's coming next.

"Kayla, you go and get washed up for dinner," Aunt Jeanie orders.

"Yes, Auntie." I was hoping she'd be cooking. *I am starving!*

"Sally Walker!" Aunt Jeanie calls. "You come down here right now."

Quickly I wash my hands and face and rush back into the kitchen. I don't want to miss Sally getting in trouble after she said *I'm* the one who started it. Sally slowly steps down the stairs and sits, pouting like a six-year-old.

"Young lady," Aunt Jeanie begins, "you have guests until the end of the summer, and I will not have you carrying on like this."

"Mom, Kayla is the one who started it!" Sally says, pointing at me. *See?* "She signed me up for double

Dutch and I don't want to be on any stupid double Dutch team!"

Wait a minute, hold the ropes! Did she just call double Dutch *stupid*?

"It's because of those white girls you let push you around," I say, very matter-of-fact.

"Kayla, honey." Aunt Jeanie turns to me. "We don't refer to people by color around this house. It's impolite and unacceptable. So please be mindful of that, okay?" I didn't mean to sound ignorant, but in my part of the neighborhood white people are like aliens—they don't come around, but we know they're out there.

"I'm sorry, Auntie." I truly respect and accept my aunt's wishes. "But she let those girls punk her. I wasn't going to just stand there and let them."

"Do you want to tell her, or should I?" Aunt Jeanie asks Sally, as if there's some big secret. Sally shrugs, still mad. "Sally used to be a Bouncing Belle, and they had a chance to showcase their team in New York."

"You mean at the Garden?" I ask. *What?* Now my ears are wide like Dumbo's.

"Yes, that's the one," Aunt Jeanie continues. "The big competition here in Charlotte was their last chance to be Junior champions, but, uh . . ."

"I froze!" Sally bursts. "I froze, okay? We never made it

58

to New York! There! Now you know why the Bouncing Belles hate me! Their chance to be champions was messed up, and it was all my fault." *Oooh.* Yeah, I probably would have been mad at her too.

"And ever since then, they haven't been very nice to Sally." Aunt Jeanie is a little upset as well. "To the point where I almost called each of their parents to give them a piece of my mind, but Sally made me vow not to. She wants to deal with this on her own."

"Well, now you have a chance to show them what you're about," I say, crossing my arms.

"What are you talking about?" Sally asks in an agitated voice. "I'm not jumping double Dutch ever again."

"You have to," I tell her. "Last I remember, you loved double Dutch *and* you were good. Besides, I signed your name on the list for double Dutch jumpers. We start tomorrow." I smile like I did a good thing.

"Why did you do that?" Sally is angrier now.

"Because it's time you stood up for yourself, that's why!" I'm now acting like the older-cousin-by-five-months that I am.

"You can't make me!" Sally yells.

"Fine," I say defiantly. "Then let those bullies run over you whenever they want." I didn't mean to make Sally cry, but she does. Seeing this makes me think she's really hurt and probably has been for a long time. "I'm sorry," I say as she covers her face. "But, Sally, it's either you let them get the best of you or you finally get them off your back."

"Sally, I think it's a good idea," Aunt Jeanie agrees. "You don't have anything to prove to anyone, but to stand up for yourself, continue doing something you love and not let anyone stop you. I'm all for that."

Sally shakes her head and stands up. "You," she commands, pointing to me, "come with me!"

Now what? *Finally the competitive cousin I remember is starting to return.* I follow her to her room as Aunt Jeanie throws her hands up and mumbles to herself: "I guess what Mom says isn't cool, but I know I'm right. Bullying my child, please." *She's so funny.*

Sally flies down the hall to her bedroom, the same room I haven't been invited into until now. So whatever she wants to show me must be important. And of course her room looks like a dark pink unicorn exploded from a secret treasure chest that belonged to a leprechaun. I mean, glittery things are everywhere—blinged-out pillows, old ballet slippers hanging on the closet door, S-A-L-L-Y spelled out on a shelf in old Broadway lights. *Okay, that's pretty cool.* She immediately starts typing on her computer until a website from the Netherlands pops up with a picture of a white guy jumping single rope.

"Who's that?" I ask.

"That's Ivy's grandfather. Double Dutch is in her blood," Sally says. "Ivy comes from a long line of jump rope champions."

"And?" I ask. "What does that have to do with you and the way they treat you? Because you messed up?"

"You don't get it?" Sally explains, "These girls eat, drink, and sleep double Dutch. That's all they do, that's all they ever dream about." *So they're kind of like me.* "And I made their team because I did too."

"And what about now?" I ask.

"I mean, I miss it, of course," Sally admits. "But . . ."

"But what? Jump!" I insist. "Who cares what they think?"

"But you don't know these girls. They can *really* jump." Sally is trying to convince herself that she's not good enough. *She has got to stop this!*

"They can't be that good," I say. "They live in the South." She stares at me.

"You have so much to learn," she says, shaking her head. What? *Do I sound ignorant again?*

"Come on!" Sally leaves the room, expecting me to follow. I don't know what she's up to, but she sure is going to every end to show me why she's scared of these girls. Suddenly Cameron and my little cousins yell and run past us in the hall and down the stairs.

"Cameron!" I call. He stops for a second and looks at

me, then continues running. "Are you behaving yourself or do I have to call Mommy?"

"Yes!" He runs off, giggling. "Uncle Larry called us to pick weeds. If we find worms, he's going to take us fishing!" This from a boy who couldn't find his socks if they were snakes. Well, he must be having a good time if he's giddy over picking weeds and worms. And his tablet is nowhere in sight. I'm glad one of us is having fun. I catch up with Sally, hoping I can still convince her to jump again.

Before we can get completely out the door, Aunt Jeanie calls to us to be back in for dinner in a half hour. I'm tempted to see what she's cooking, but Sally pulls me out the door. *What is this girl up to?*

Next thing I know, Sally's got me crossing streets, running through people's backyards, and climbing a fence full of bushes. *Bugs!* I feel like they're attacking me from every direction. *I hate bugs!* I might have even swallowed a few gnats. *Yuck!* Finally we are peeking through the bushes in front of a huge, beautiful house, kind of like my cousin's, but this one is a little more countrified.

"What are we doing?" I whisper, and swat away flies.

"I want you to see what I'm talking about. Look!" Sally whispers back, pointing through the bushes to the backyard. I look and am amazed. She's right. These girls can *jump*! They are doing gymnastics in the ropes, backflips, double team dancing—tricks I've never seen before. *This is crazy!* Never in a million years would I have thought Southern girls could jump double Dutch like that. I've heard rumors about some kids trying, but not like this! I guess because I hadn't seen it with my own eyes. But my friends were right: there *are* double Dutch teams that can be just as good as New York teams. *My mind is shattered right now.*

Buzz! A bee!

"Aaaaah!" I scream, and swat at it wildly.

One of the girls hears me and looks up suspiciously. We try to hurry and get off the fence and out of the bushes, but we can't move fast enough. Sally and I roll out of the bushes and onto the ground. In seconds, we're surrounded by Bouncing Belles.

Ivy laughs. "Well, if it isn't loser Sally Walker and her tomboy cousin."

"Who are you calling a loser?" I say, getting to my feet. And did she call me a tomboy?

"Were you guys spying on us?" the Asian girl, even smaller than Ivy, asks. "That's just creepy."

"I was just showing my cousin, uh, how . . . ," Sally tries to explain.

"How great we are?" Ivy says, smiling at the Belles.

"We know we are, and without you on our team we're even better."

"No. My cousin was showing me how lame you are." I get in her face. "And for your information, I'm from Brooklyn, and some of the best double Dutch jumpers are from Brooklyn. So as far as I can see, you ain't got nothing on me." What was I supposed to say? You guys are, like, so good. I want to be on your team. *Not happening.*

"Well, where's your team?" Ivy folds her arms, looking around. "Last I checked, there's only the two of you, and you need four for a team in Charlotte, 'Brooklyn.' " This girl is cruising for a bruising.

"Don't worry about what we're doing," I cover. "You just keep working on your little weak tricks, Southern Belle. You'll get to New York someday." I walk away, tugging Sally, who seems to be stuck in a trance.

"You better not steal any of our moves," Ivy calls as we walk away.

"Wasn't planning on it," I call back. I have to put up a front. There's no way I can let these girls think that I'm threatened by their skills. Especially with my cousin watching, who looks riddled with fear. Even if I have to fake my courage, they will never know I am the slightest bit impressed. It's just another little thing I learned growing up in Brooklyn. *We New Yorkers are hard to impress.*

"Thanks," Sally says softly.

"For what?" I ask.

"For standing up to them," she replies.

"Sally, the only reason why they bully you is because you let them." I stop her in the middle of the empty street. "I know it might be hard to stand up for yourself, but as long as I'm here, I've got your back." I can tell by the look on her face that she isn't sure she can trust what I'm saying, but I mean it. "They're probably afraid of you because you're as good as or even better than they are. Why do you think they checked to see if your name was on the list?" Sally seems to ponder this. "It's up to you now. Are you going to back down, or are you going to prove to yourself that you deserve to be respected?"

Sally doesn't answer, but I can tell she's thinking about it. I hope she pulls it together, because I am not losing to some "Belles" who think they can jump better than I can. I run ahead—Auntie's cooking is waiting.

Two Times Two

Something must have clicked in Sally's mind, because she's up early banging on my door to make sure I'm getting ready for camp. Once we're there, announcements are made that teams must be submitted by the end of the day, and if there aren't enough names to make a team, then "those individuals will be placed in large group sports like baseball, soccer, and so forth." Panic sets in, and Sally and I run to check our list to see if anyone signed up for our team. Nobody did.

"Man! Isn't there anybody else who can jump double Dutch around here?" I ask.

"Hi, girls," a Barbie-type counselor interrupts. "I'm

Kirsten, the head coach for double Dutch." *Really?* She's so, um, perky, more like a cheerleader, but I'm totally judging. "Are you guys looking for girls for your double Dutch team?"

"Yes." Sally steps up. "Do you know anybody?"

"No, and as far as I know, the girls who can jump already have their teams made up—you know what I mean?" *Uh, no.* "I just thought I'd suggest hurrying to get into one of the other group sports or you might be out of luck." *Well, that's kind of rude.* If she was anything like my coach, Ms. Jackson, she would've figured something out. I've never seen her turn anybody away.

"We have until the end of the day, right?" I ask.

"Well, yeah, but it might be hard finding someone at this point, so, yeah?" Kirsten says doubtfully. *Who is this lady, Negative Nancy?*

Just then, the Belles enter the gym. Gesturing to Sally, they all pantomime like they're going to jump a double Dutch rope, then freeze. Suddenly they laugh, then run to Coach Kirsten. Hmm, I see she has her favorites.

"We'll submit a team before the end of the day," Sally says to Kirsten through gritted teeth, staring at the Belles. *Okay, Sally's really in now.* The counselor shrugs and just walks away. *Oh yeah, it's on!* But where are we going to find jumpers in such a short time?

Sally and I devise a plan to find the best candidates for

our soon-to-be team. First we check the list of available kids willing to be a part of any team. They are probably kids whose parents made them go to camp, whether they wanted to or not. I'm not judging, but what kid is not interested in sports—artsy theater lovers, maybe? In any case, all those kids are crossed off, meaning they found a team to take them in. *Ugh!*

"What do we do now?" says Sally, concerned. "It doesn't look like anyone's left." I think for a second, then . . .

"What happens if someone doesn't work out?" I wonder.

"What do you mean?" Sally asks.

"Come on, follow me," I order, then run out of the gym. "I have an idea."

We search around the camp, one sport after another. Counselors or coaches are testing their players to place them in the right positions on the teams.

"Just because kids are put on teams doesn't mean they're going to work out," I tell Sally as we scout the fields. "Look for anyone, boy or girl, who doesn't seem like they're going to be even put in the game for their team."

"Why would we want that person on *our* team?" Sally asks.

"Because we're desperate," I say emphatically.

"True," Sally says, resigned. "Boys too?"

"Boys in Japan, China, and Denmark jump double Dutch . . . more than girls, so I've heard," I state.

"Really?" Sally says incredulously.

"It's actually making American boys step up to the plate," I inform her.

We're even searching the skateboard ramps. As far as I can see, I doubt there's any guy who would remotely be interested in double Dutch. Then—

Wham! This boy on a skateboard knocks me off my feet!

"Did you *not* see me?" I yell at him.

"I'm sorry." He helps me up. *Really?* "I thought you were going to move out of the way."

"*Eeng!*" I make the sound of a buzzer. "Wrong! Watch where you're going next time," I say, dusting myself off.

The boy smirks, then skates off.

"That. Was. Charlie. Davis." Sally is mesmerized.

"Who?" I take it she knows him.

"Only the cutest guy in Charlotte," she says.

"Whatever," I say. *He is kind of cute, though.* The boy looks back again and smiles.

"Uh!" Sally gasps. "I think he likes you."

"What?"

"It figures." Sally sulks a little. "It baffles me that boys from here like girls who are, um . . . have New York style." *Did she just diss me?*

"What's that supposed to mean?" I ask. First some double Dutch bully calls me a tomboy, and now my cousin thinks there's something different about my swagger. Okay, so I'm not dressed like some girlie-girl or prima donna. Not that that's a bad thing; it's just not my style.

"Nothing. Forget it," Sally insists. "Let's just keep looking."

Although she waves it off, I suddenly feel funny about how I'm dressed. Are my Mets jersey and jeans giving people the wrong impression? In my neighborhood, you have to always appear tough and have a strong attitude. If you don't, people will think you're weak and pick on you, plain and simple.

Sally and I check every track-and-field player for potential double Dutch jumpers, but it's getting late in the day, and everyone seems to be pretty set on teams. I begin to worry.

"What about the baseball fields?" Sally asks.

"Let's go!" At this point, beggars can't be choosers.

We run to the baseball diamonds, and even the outfielders who can't catch a pop fly don't want to join us. Some guys laugh at us for even asking. We get rejected by some kids who couldn't hit a tennis ball if it was the size of a basketball. I think at least the swim teams will have somebody who can't swim, but no. They look at us like we have six heads, and like double Dutch is the name of some yucky ice cream.

That's it, we're done. Sally looks kind of sad, but I can tell by the way she is swinging her arms and almost skipping that she is trying to play it off like she's not. Maybe she is relieved that she won't have to compete against those Bouncing Belles. I keep looking around, hoping we'll find someone, so she can stand up to them. Just then we hear a girl cursing up a storm as we pass the soccer field. Sally and I stop to check it out. A burly girl who is supposed to be playing goalie on a soccer team is being outworked by every soccer ball she misses. They whiz past her hands every time. She's cursing as if it's the ball's fault for slipping through her hands. The coach reprimands her for cursing, but she curses him out too. He blows a whistle and orders her off the field.

"Looks like we found our first teammate," I say, and take off toward the girl.

"But she's—she's . . . big . . . and angry!" Sally says fearfully.

"All the better!" I yell back to Sally.

Once I reach the girl, she kicks dirt unknowingly right in our direction. After I fan the cloud of dust out of my face, I can tell she's freckle-faced, with thick, curly sandy-blond hair, and she looks like she can knock down anyone who gets in her way. I bet she would make a better catcher on a softball team, but her muscular arms just might make her a great turner. She's perfect for our double Dutch team. I let her cool off for a second. As my daddy would say, "You don't want to poke a snake when it's rattling its tail." I never really understood what he meant until now. Sally catches up.

"Seriously?" Sally asks. The girl overhears and turns around.

"What the hell you looking at?" she says. Sally starts to walk away. I pull her back.

"Um, hi, I'm Kayla, and this is my cousin Sally." I fake a smile. "We're looking for a couple of girls who'd like to be on our double Dutch team."

"Do I look like a girl who plays double Dutch? What the hell is that, anyway?" she says with a thick Southern accent. I take it by the way this girl talks that she's allowed to curse in her house.

"It's like jump rope, but with two ropes," Sally chimes in. "It's fun. Maybe it'll help you with your . . . uh, situation?" Is Sally trying to tell this girl she's fat? I elbow her and give her a look.

"I think you'd be good for double Dutch." I smile again. "What's your name?"

"Melissa," she answers. "What's it to ya?"

"Well, I think you'd make a great turner. I mean, you have some big guns." I do a muscle pose.

"Sure, you're right." Melissa flexes her muscles. "I've got four brothers who make me pump iron with them. I can even do ten straight push-ups. Wanna see?" Before we can answer, Melissa drops and gives us ten. Sally's eyes squint like she's seeing something gross. I think it's great a girl her size can do at least one push-up.

"Well, that's—" Sally starts.

"Nice!" I interrupt whatever dumb thing is going to fly out of Sally's mouth.

"Hey, in this double Dutch thing, will I have to catch or kick anything? Because this soccer crap is for the birds."

"No, but we'll have to find one more person for us to have a team," I tell her. "If we don't, the camp is going to place us wherever they want." Melissa looks around and thinks for a moment, then throws down the catching gloves.

"To hell with this. Come on!" Melissa says.

"Great!" I'm so excited I could hug her. Then Melissa runs off.

"Let's go kick some double Dutch butt!" Melissa yells back.

"Her? Really?" Sally asks me with an incredulous look on her face. "She knows nothing about double Dutch."

"Do you have a better choice?"

"I say we keep looking."

"Come on, let's go get my friend Tina. She'll join our team!" Melissa calls back.

"Cool!" I yell. "Sally, let's just go with it and see. All she'll have to do is turn the ropes." I try to kill the pessimism. "We'll do the rest. Let's just try. Come on!" I run to catch up with Melissa. Sally finally trots along.

We head over to the outdoor basketball courts, where girls are practicing for the basketball team. Melissa points to a girl on the court. This girl is shorter and skinnier than Melissa, with brown skin and long dark hair. I think she's Latina, but I know one thing—that girl couldn't dribble a ball if her life depended on it. She bounces it too low, then too high, then the ball finally hits her in the face. She also has earbuds in that are attached to her phone. She must be listening to music, because she surely isn't listening to the coaches as they direct her for a layup. The ball doesn't even come close to the hoop. Not even halfway up the pole. *Wow! She's bad.* Sally smacks herself in the head.

"Please don't say that's her," Sally groans. "That girl has no coordination. Introducing her to double Dutch is going to be like asking for a train wreck."

"Well, she's fearless. I'll give her that." I smirk.

Melissa skips onto the court and pulls her friend aside. The Latina takes out her earbuds, then quickly drops the ball and runs off the court with Melissa. The coach acts like she's upset but wipes her forehead in relief and quickly turns back to the others doing the exercise.

Melissa introduces the short girl with butterfingers. "Hey, you guys, this is my best friend, Tina. Tina, this is Kayla and Sally."

"Hi," Sally and I say simultaneously.

"*¡Hola!*" Tina says. "*¿Que pasa?*" Okay, this might be difficult if she *only* speaks Spanish.

"We need another member for our double Dutch team," Melissa says, all in.

"That sounds way more fun than this basketball stuff," Tina says. Relieved she speaks English, I smile at her.

"I think you're going to like it," I add. Suddenly the coach does her duty and calls to Tina to rejoin the group.

"I'm outta here!" Tina and Melissa run off, laughing. Oh my gosh! *Did she just flip the bird to the coach?* My impression of Southern girls has just been completely shattered. Now I am learning why my mother tells me not to be so quick to judge people before I know the whole story.

"Really?" Sally looks at me. I don't have an answer, so I shrug and run after Melissa and Tina.

"Let's go! We have to sign up before it's too late!" I say as I motion for my cousin to hurry.

We haul back to the gym to put our names in. As we enter, I see the scratchy-voice lady closing the registration window, and we call for her to wait. Melissa and Tina sign their names under our double Dutch list, but then I realize . . .

"We need a name for our team," I say as I look to them for suggestions.

"How about Best Damn Double Dutch Crew Ever?" Melissa says.

"We can't have curses in the title," Sally says.

"What about All That Double Dutch Team?" Tina adds.

"Not bad," I answer. "All that" is *so* outdated, but I don't want to crush her enthusiasm.

"How about Mixed Nuts?" Sally says sarcastically. The scratchy-voice lady behind the window is getting impatient as she looks at her watch, then back at us.

"Forget it, we'll come up with one later," I say as I write "TBD" and hand in the sheet. It's official. We have a team and we're in!

Afterward we celebrate. Well, everyone but Sally. We turn around to see other girls already in the gym jumping double Dutch, including the Bouncing Belles. Lucky for us, we missed the exhibition to show our skills. Right now I don't even know if we all actually *have* any skills as a team. Coach Kirsten sees us watching and trots over.

"So did you guys find a team?" she asks.

"You're looking at it," I say with pride. She gives us an odd look. Our clothes are all dusty from the soccer field, and the heat and humidity have wreaked havoc on our hair. We are a mess, and to make matters worse Melissa stares at the double Dutch teams with her jaw dropped; Tina has gone back to rocking out to a Spanish song on her phone. As for Sally, she just stares at the floor, embarrassed.

"Okay then," Coach Kirsten says. "Since there's only a few more minutes left, why don't you guys come on over and show us what you've got?"

I try to cover smoothly. "Uh, my cousin and I just got here, so we kind of need some time to work on our routine with our new team."

"Yeah, a *lot* of time, 'cause that stuff looks complicated," Melissa blurts out.

"That's double Dutch, right?" Tina yells, not realizing how loud she is with her earbuds in. The counselor gives us the side-eye as Sally and I look at each other, not knowing how to save face.

"Sure, take your time," Coach Kirsten says. "Uh, tomorrow is group activities with the camp. So make sure you're ready to go on Monday, all right?"

We all agree as she saunters away. *Thank goodness!* We may look like an oddball crew, but we're a team. And we have three days to literally show Melissa and Tina the ropes. But before I can grab a pair of ropes, the bell sounds. Camp is over!

Meeting the Boys

I figure if we don't get started now, we're doomed. So instead of going home after camp, Sally and I call Aunt Jeanie on Tina's phone to ask if she'll let us hang out with Melissa and Tina for practice. She says yes but to be home before sunset. *Cool!* The stuffy camp won't let us borrow double Dutch ropes, so we decide to go buy one. Melissa and Tina agree to take us on their bikes to the nearest hardware store, where I am sure we can find some kind of rope to turn with.

Tina gives me her bike, then jumps on the two pegs on the back wheel of Melissa's bike, placing her hands on Melissa's shoulders. She's going to ride like that?

"I've never ridden a bike like that before," I say apprehensively.

"And I thought you city girls knew how to do everything." Sally grabs the handlebars and hops on, gesturing for me to do the same as Tina. I get on and grab Sally's shoulders for dear life.

Finally we're off.

Riding through the neighborhoods with manicured lawns and colorful flowers, I see houses that remind me of the picture books I read to Cameron. Some houses make me think of the drawings in old social studies textbooks of Colonial homes built in the 1800s. Although back then only white folks lived in them. Here, it seems, there are all kinds of neighbors living harmoniously side by side. I don't think I would've believed it if I wasn't seeing it with my own eyes. It makes me wonder if people are stuck in the way things used to be in the South. Does racism really exist like I've seen in the news? Hmm, by the looks of this neighborhood, I'm not so sure. As the wind blows through my braids, I suddenly feel . . . calm, safe. It's weird—the quietness doesn't bother me anymore. It's kind of nice. I guess living in New York City makes me feel like that's all there is to life: concrete, honking horns, and the constant noise of everyone's busyness. I'm not saying I'd live here or anything—there are way too many bugs with wings and things—but maybe that little old lady on the plane was right when she said, *Charlotte is wonderful in the summertime.*

Finally we arrive at a local hardware store way across town. I guess those bigger lumberjack stores are probably off a highway or somewhere you can't ride bikes to. This little place should have what we need. To my surprise, Sally and Melissa park the bikes outside without locks or anything.

"Aren't you guys afraid someone's going to steal them?" I ask. "Where I come from, you can't just leave your bike. Someone will snatch it up as soon as you turn your back. I'll just go in and get the rope."

"They'll be fine," Sally reassures me. "You're in the South, remember? We do things differently round these parts." Is she mocking me?

"I dare someone to take my bike," Melissa grunts. "I'd hunt them down like a bloodhound."

"And she will too. *Esta loca.*" Tina laughs.

"Well, all right," I say. *'Nough said.* I mean, a street with only two lanes, one stoplight, and trees up and down the block doesn't seem like the sort of place where much of anything happens.

The little store is so quiet you can hear the electricity in the old fluorescent lightbulbs, and the rickety wood floors smell like there's mold lurking under them. It's as if I've stepped back in time to the Civil War and all that's missing is the Confederate flag. No, hold the phone, there's one on the counter. Suddenly those safe feelings from earlier just disappear, and my New York senses kick in; or maybe I'm scared. I want to get the rope and get the heck out of here. No one's at the register, but the rest of the girls, including Sally, don't seem to be nervous.

"Can I help you ladies?" a raspy voice says with a deep Southern accent. We all jump and turn around to find a white-bearded old man wearing a cap and talking out of the side of his mouth.

"We're just here to pick up some rope," I say quickly, and stare back. I don't know why I am so scared. I think it's the flag. It's like a big yellow traffic sign that says CAUTION—POSSIBLE RACIST AHEAD! I remember the news reports on how people in South Carolina were complaining about what it represents. One side thinks it says hatred of black people. The other side says it's Southern pride. Either way, it doesn't make me feel welcome in this creepy little store that smells like old, wet wood. I see the rope and grab one that looks about the right length.

"What do you need with a clothesline? You girls plan on doing an awful lot of laundry?" he says, snatching the rope out of my hand to check the price. "Either that or tying somebody up." He laughs, but no, that's not funny.

"Yeah, we plan on tying somebody up," Tina snaps sarcastically. "People automatically think of laundry when they see girls buying rope. Like we don't have dryers at home." *Whoa!* I'm guessing she's dealt with sarcastic old men before, or maybe the Confederate flag has put her on guard as well. Personally I thought the man would take her comment to be disrespectful, but he doesn't. He just laughs.

"Feisty little one, aintcha?" He laughs again.

"Tina, we're buying a clothesline, duh? What's anyone to think?" Melissa tries to cool Tina's jets. Or maybe Melissa doesn't have a dryer at home.

"I'm just joshin' with ya'z anyhow." The old man peers over his reading glasses as he rings us up. "Y'all making a tree house or somethin'?" Now he's just being nosy.

"No, sir," Melissa answers. "We fixin'a jump some double Dutch." What the heck is *fixin'a*?

"Double Dutch?" He seems amused. "I don't know what that is, but it sure sounds fun."

"Yessir, it's some fancier way of skipping rope is all," Melissa responds, with a heavier Southern accent than I've heard from her. I'm wondering if that's how you're supposed to relate to old-timer Southern folk. I might be right, because now it seems Melissa is the only one the man sees.

"Well, I'll be darned. That means y'all will be playing

outside like when I was a kid. That's aw'right," he says as he searches for and rustles a paper bag. "I can't remember the last time I saw young girls skipping rope. Your generation is usually sittin' in the house, playin' them vidya games or something or other on them darn cellyur phones. And they wonder why they're fat." He laughs. Melissa's smile turns upside down as she takes his comment personally. She snatches the rope off the counter and walks away.

"Wait a minute now." He stops. "Who's paying for that there merchandise?"

"I am." I quickly dig into my pocket and pull out some of the money my dad gave me.

"Well, ain't you cute as a button," he says. "I don't remember seeing you round these parts." I shoot Sally a look. *I swear, I feel like I'm in an old Western movie.* I don't say anything. Sally moves in to get the change.

"Thank you kindly, sir." She throws on this heavy Southern accent that suits her all too well. "This is my cousin. She's from New York. You know how those Yankees can be sometimes." *Is Sally selling me out?* She whispers to me, without her accent, "Some Southerners are stuck in a time warp. Just smile and let's get out of here." I do as she says as we walk to the exit. I was right—there is some sort of code way of relating to the old-timers.

"People are nosy and always trying to be so nice down here," I say to Sally.

"It's called Southern hospitality," Sally retorts.

"Well, I think it's phony," I respond.

"Of course you would—you're from New York," Sally sneers. *Okay, touché, Princess.*

When we get outside, Melissa and Tina are in shock. Their bikes are gone. They check around the corner and reappear without them.

"¡*Ay dios mío!* Somebody stole our bikes!" Tina cries.

"I told y'all." *Did I just say "y'all"?* "I knew it! Now what are we gonna do?" I am not asking that creepy man in the store to give us a ride home. Us, him, and all this rope—*uh-uh, not happening.*

A loud whistle comes from across the street. When I look, I see it's Skateboard Boy from day camp. *The cute one.* He and his friends are standing in a park with Melissa's and Tina's bikes.

"Charlie," Sally says breathlessly.

"You know this guy?" Melissa is steaming. "He's got our bikes!"

"And if he doesn't give 'em back, he's going to have to answer to my *papi*," Tina adds.

"And my brothers," Melissa says.

Melissa and Tina take off running across the street. Sally and I shrug at each other and follow them.

In seconds we are face to face with Charlie and three of his boys. The bikes are parked under a tree. Melissa is in Charlie's face.

"Those are our bikes, and we want them back!" Melissa charges.

"Slow your roll, girl." Charlie backs up.

"That's right, stop playing," Tina demands.

"Oh, I thought one of those bikes belonged to her." Charlie points to me. Suddenly my stomach sinks. "If you want your bikes back, she needs to apologize for bumping into me today at camp."

"What are you talking about? You got in my way!" I press toward Charlie as Melissa moves out of the way.

"How about it was both of our faults, but you never said you were sorry," Charlie says as he invades my space. He tilts his chin up and stares down at me. I don't know why I am thinking this right now, but this boy is sooooo cute! What the heck is that? I suddenly feel like someone is tickling my stomach, and I am very ticklish. *Butterflies?* I've only read stories about boys and butterflies in some teen magazine. I just thought they were making that stuff up. *And* he's acting like a jerk right now, in a weird sort of curious way. I have to pull it together quickly. I don't want my new friends to think I'm a punk, even though he's the cutest boy I've seen in my life.

"You better get out of my face," I say. He moves in even

closer. *OMG! Is he going to kiss me?* I can't help but stare at his lips. They're right in front of my eyes.

"Go ahead, take 'em," his lips say. I can't think. I am mesmerized by his lips. They are so . . . close. *What was I asking him, anyway?* Suddenly I just push him away and go for the bikes. He quickly grabs the packaged rope out of my hand, which I completely forgot I even had. I reach for the rope, but he pulls back.

"What's wrong with you, boy? Give me the rope," I demand. Melissa joins in and tries to grab it from the boys, who are now passing it away from us.

"Stop acting like a dumbass and give it to me!" Melissa almost scares the pants off this one boy who is half her size, but he tosses the rope before she can get to him. Suddenly we girls are forced into a game of monkey in the middle. The boys taunt us with every throw. After a few rounds of them making us look like fools, I spot their football. I go for it.

"You wanna play?" I taunt. They all turn and look at me like I'm crazy. Now I have their ball *and* their attention. "We win and you give us our rope and we'll give you your ball back. We lose and you keep the rope. Deal?" I propose with attitude. The boys snicker. "Our ball." I smile.

"Charlie, what's up with this, man? We can't hit girls," one of the boys says with a lisp.

87

"Of course not," Charlie says. "No worries, fellas, this is going to be a cakewalk."

"Mmm . . . cake," one boy says.

Sally runs over to me in a panic. I turn to face my team, who're looking at me like I'm crazy.

"What are you doing?" Sally whispers. "We don't know how to play football."

"Hold on, let me think," I say as I contemplate my plan.

Even though my dad isn't my favorite person right now, I do remember him giving me a lesson about boys over dinner one time when I was in fourth grade. This boy kept pulling my hair and tapping me on the shoulder and then hiding. My dad said that boys will do foolish things to get a girl's attention. And that since boys have a hard time expressing themselves, it's up to the girl to show that she's a lady and that foolishness is unacceptable. My mother said that a girl can get a boy to do anything she wants if he really likes her. It's part of our "girl power," she explained.

My dad said the trick for the girl is to see how far a boy is willing to keep making a fool of himself, because when she finally does give him the time of day, she will feel that he's earned it.

Well, I know that it was all Cute Boy Charlie's idea to take our bikes, so this might be Charlie's foolish thing.

"If he wants my attention, he's got it," I say aloud.

"What are you talking about?" Sally is clueless.

"You'll see," I assure her. "Come on." The boys look at me incredulously, as do Sally and Tina. But not Melissa; she looks like she's ready to go.

"I don't know how to play football," Tina insists.

"Neither do I," Sally says.

"Neither do I," I add. "But I've watched enough football with my dad and little brother to know that all you gotta do is—"

"Get the ball and put it in the end zone!" Melissa interrupts. "I have four brothers and a gridiron in my backyard." Melissa is seriously ready to take some guys out. "Let's do this!" She smashes her fist into her hand. *Okay, she's scaring me now.* "Come on, huddle up!" We grab each other at the shoulders and huddle almost out of fear of Melissa.

"So what are we going to do?" Sally asks.

"All right, listen up," I tell them. "Melissa, I want you to help me get the ball, and then I'll get it to Sally."

"Why me?" asks Sally. "Why do I get the ball?"

Melissa sizes Sally up. "Because you're the smallest and you can probably run really fast."

"Well, I did run track in fifth grade," Sally admits.

"Be ready when I hike the ball," Melissa says to me.

"Gotcha!" I say. "And while Melissa and I block two of the boys, Tina, you do something to distract the other two."

"Like what?" asks Tina. "I don't know what . . . wait, I know what to do. I got this!" Tina seems like she can figure her way in or out of anything.

"Good," I say, reassured.

"And, Sally, as soon as you get the ball, run like hell! *Capisce?*" Melissa pats Sally on the back harder than she can stand. Sally squints in pain. I hold back from laughing.

"Are you guys going to have a pajama party or are we going to play football?" Charlie yells from the other side of the field.

"We can do this, you guys!" Melissa says with encouragement.

"Girl power on three," I say. "One-two-three!"

"Girl power!" we exclaim.

We hear the boys laughing at us as we get into formation—maybe not so neatly, but it is good enough. I look into Charlie's big brown eyes as Melissa leans over for the ball.

"You guys are going down," Melissa says, staring at the boy facing her. He pretends to shake a bit, then smiles sarcastically.

"Ready, hike!" I yell.

Melissa throws the ball high, but I quickly catch it and run until Charlie grabs me around the waist. *Hey! Can he do that?* I toss the ball to Sally, who bounces it around like a hot potato. Once she gets a good grip, she runs while Melissa tries to tackle two boys at once, but one gets away and chases after Sally. Melissa wrestles the other to the ground and holds him with all her might. I look up to see Tina just talking to one boy while she loosens her hair and flips it back and forth. The boy has on a goofy smile and seems hypnotized. *Way to go, Tina!* I guess she's already learned how to use her girl power. I break away from Charlie, who has been holding on to me way too long, and watch Sally outrun the boy on her trail. She takes off like a lightning bolt into the end zone. We celebrate!

"Yes!" I scream.

"So long, losers," Melissa taunts.

"I think I like football," Tina says sarcastically. "We should do this more often!" Sally shoves the football into Charlie's gut and smiles at him. She gives me a high five. It's cool to see her happy about the challenge. I grab the rope off the grass while Melissa and Tina gather their bikes. Sally and I hop onto the backs and leave the boys in the dust. As we ride away, we take one last look at the boys and give them the L sign. I think Melissa shows them her middle finger. *Oh well, that's her.* All they can do is shake their heads. Even Charlie cracks a smile at me. Sally sees this and looks at me funny. I give her a look like, *What?* Okay, he may be cute, but he's obnoxious and rude, like Daddy said he would be. All I know is we dusted those guys!

As we roll up to Sally's house, we're still laughing about beating the boys at their own game and don't notice how dark it has become. Suddenly Aunt Jeanie is standing in the doorway with her arms crossed. Uh-oh, she does not look happy.

New Leaf

Melissa and Tina nearly dump us onto the lawn and hightail it up the street. It looks like Aunt Jeanie is breathing so hard steam is coming out of her nose. I am just hoping fire isn't going to come out of her mouth, but no such luck.

"Do you both know what time it is?" Aunt Jeanie points at her watch.

I guess we were having so much fun that we completely forgot about the time.

"Sally, your father is out there looking all around for y'all," Aunt Jeanie continues as we walk through the doors with our heads down. "You know better than this."

"But, Ma—" Sally starts.

"It was my fault," I interrupt. "We went to buy some rope for double Dutch and—"

Aunt Jeanie cuts me off. "Honey, no need to explain. Whatever y'all need, you just let me know." She simmers down a bit, *thank goodness*. I almost tell her how we had to get the rope back from a bunch of boys by beating them in a football game. But all she would hear is that we were playing with a bunch of boys, and then her head probably would explode. "I just don't want y'all roaming the streets and nobody knowing where you are. These neighborhoods may look safe, but I need to know where you are at all times," Aunt Jeanie continues with a long, chilling stare.

I must admit, as much as I hate being reprimanded, I appreciate that somebody cares about my whereabouts. Even if I think I can take care of myself, it's nice to know someone is looking after me. I just hope this doesn't mean I have to go to sleep without dinner. *I'm hungry.*

I try to get back into this master chef's good graces. "Um, Aunt Jeanie, is there anything to eat?"

"If you all promise not to do this ever again, I might let you have something to eat," she says. Then, through the side of her mouth, "Running my blood pressure through the roof."

"We promise," Sally and I say in unison.

"All right, you all get washed up and I'll warm you some supper," Aunt Jeanie says with a delayed smirk. "Your uncle took the boys down to the river this afternoon and caught a boatload of fish." *Cool!* I think she's truly relieved that we're in the house. *Who says "supper" anymore?*

After my shower, I quickly check on Cameron in Michael and Eddie's bedroom. I'm guessing the fishing trip wore him out, because he and my little cousins are already fast asleep on the floor with video game controllers in their hands. He actually has a smile on his face. I don't think I've ever seen Cameron sleeping before seven o'clock. He may get on my nerves sometimes, but he's really a good kid. *Roar!* Was that my stomach? I quietly shut the door and quickly head to the kitchen. Supper smells good! Sally and I sit there in our pajamas and wolf down Aunt Jeanie's catfish and yummy corn bread. Man, my aunt can cook!

Even though we had a fun afternoon, I don't even know if Melissa and Tina will turn out to be any good at double Dutch. But I don't want to lose the opportunity to compete, even if we look like fools jumping around in the gym. I guess we'll figure it out tomorrow, but I know one thing: today was more fun than I thought I would have here in the South.

Finally Sally and I put our dishes in the sink and walk

upstairs. Sally stands at her door for a second, then turns around.

"I'm glad we found a team," Sally whispers. "Now I'll be able to show the Belles they've made a mistake by shutting me out."

"I just hope Melissa and Tina will be as good at double Dutch as they were at football," I snicker.

"Today was so fun!" she says as she looks back to see if her parents' door is closed. It is. She gestures for me to come to her room. I tiptoe across the hall, and we run and jump onto the bed with two feet.

"Did you see how Melissa pinned that one boy?" Sally laughs. "He didn't have a chance."

"You should've seen Tina." I laugh back. "She had that boy like . . ." I stare with wide eyes.

"I know," Sally says. "They all looked like this when I made the touchdown." She crosses her eyes, and we jump around on the bed, laughing. Who knew my stiff little cousin Sally could be this silly? We reenact the whole game, laughing at every move the boys made. "Did you see the look on Charlie's face when—"

Suddenly the bedroom door flies open. It's Uncle Larry.

"Heeey!" he whispers loudly. "I'm happy you two are finally getting along, but y'all got the dogs barking in the neighborhood." We stare at him blankly. "Now get some sleep." We drop to the bed and giggle as he shuts the door.

"It looks like Charlie really likes you," Sally teases.

"No, he doesn't," I deny, only wishing those butterflies I felt for him were mutual.

"He does, and you know it," Sally insists. "Well, consider yourself lucky. There are a lot of girls at school who would love to be his girlfriend." *Girlfriend? Hmm, could he possibly think of me as his . . . girlfriend?* Sally pulls the covers over herself and suddenly falls silent.

I tiptoe to my room and try to fall asleep, but I just can't. I keep wondering, *Me? Charlie's girlfriend?* I find my diary as if it was waiting to hear something juicy. I smile as I feverishly write about this new boy, Charlie, and how I keep dreaming of his lips close to mine. I wonder if I'll see him tomorrow at camp and will he even say hi. . . . I hope so. Then again, we did kick their butts in football. *Ha ha!*

I wake up with a pen print and a silly grin on my face. I must've fallen asleep on my diary, thinking, *What if Sally is right? What if Charlie really likes me?* Could it be I have a crush on him? His glowing, dark tanned skin and big brown eyes, the kind that match his skin perfectly, are just so, so . . . ugh! *Butterflies.* He's so cute! I jump up, excited to get myself ready for the day. *Wait a minute.* I'm excited? Well, I did put together a double Dutch team, and there's a cute boy at my camp who my cousin thinks likes me, *and* my cousin seems to be cooler than I thought. *Crazy.* This summer can't get any better . . . *can it?*

As I get dressed, I can't help feeling like Beyoncé and JLo in the posters are staring at me, compelling me to check myself out in the mirror. I wonder if I have anything of what they have. . . . *Uh, no.* I wonder how they got so, so confident with their . . . stuff? Maybe because they have "stuff"? Were they always proud, or did they ever do like I'm doing, checking my reflection as I poke out my chest to see if there's a curve anywhere on my hips, thinking, *Am I sexy? What boy is going to go crazy over this?* I suddenly feel stupid and snap out of it. I've never stopped to think about how my body looks except for when my feet are hitting the floor in double Dutch. What does it matter if I don't have any curves? I then imagine Bey and JLo saying something like, *Maybe it's that boy you like.* I imitate their poses in the mirror, thinking, *Yeah, cute boys like girls with gifts.* Well, I may not have all the "boom-boom-pow" body parts that get a boy's attention, but if one boy likes me, I guess maybe he *already* likes what he sees. And if he doesn't, so what? We can't all be Beyoncés or JLos.

Suddenly I overhear my uncle Larry having a conversation with Sally as he works around the hole he and his crew dug for the pool. By Sally's body language I can tell she's down about something. *What's wrong now?* It seems she has a better bond with her dad than she does with my aunt Jeanie. I can understand, because Aunt Jeanie's attitude is cut-and-dried, and she doesn't like a whole lot of whining over anything. I guess I get my attitude from her and not from my mom, who's always so emotional.

I start eavesdropping a bit; okay, a lot. Anytime I hear the words "double Dutch," my ears just tune in automatically.

"I know Kayla is trying, but I don't think we have a chance at the double Dutch contest," Sally confesses to her father.

"Oh, stop that worrying," Uncle Larry says as he continues working. "Just give it your best shot."

"Dad, it's not about double Dutch." Sally sulks. "It's about when summer's over. It's . . . forget it."

"Is this about when you see those girls at school?" Uncle Larry stops for a moment. "Do you need me to go down there?"

"No, Daddy!" Sally's voice is filled with fear.

I thought she was over this and on to redeeming herself, but obviously not. Those double Dutch divas must have picked on Sally so bad that it's really put the fear in her. *Well, that's got to change.* Even if my cousin acts like a square princess sometimes, she doesn't deserve to be hated on or bullied by anyone.

"You know, when I was your age, if someone had a beef with me, it was me and that guy going mano a mano at three o'clock," Uncle Larry says.

"Dad, fighting is so barbaric," says Sally.

"Yeah, well, fighting never solved anything anyway," Uncle Larry says. "All we did was let off some steam, then later we'd become friends, and before you knew it we were down at the creek fishing like nothing ever happened. Besides, you shouldn't be fighting no ways." Sally smirks at her dad. "You never know, things can change. Look at you and your cousin," Uncle Larry continues. "I thought you two were going to kill each other before the summer was over, but you're getting along, right?"

"I guess." Sally sighs. "At first I didn't want her here, but she's been really cool, acting kind of like a big sister. But she's going to leave, and then what?"

"Well, at some point, you're going to have to stand up for yourself, honey," Uncle Larry says as he continues to clear debris. "Or else I'll have to make a few personal calls to some of them parents, you hear me?" Sally just sighs again as though she knows it's time for her to do something about it.

I smile, happy Sally sees that at least I have put our differences aside and stepped up like a big sister.

Suddenly my bedroom door flies open while I'm still dressing. I cover up with my bathrobe.

Cameron barges in. "I miss Mommy and Daddy."

"Cameron!" I yell. "Don't you know how to knock?" He looks so deflated that I can only hug him. I am *his* big sister first.

"Yeah, I miss them too, but I don't miss the fighting. Do you?" I ask. He shakes his head. "I don't miss them yelling at each other or at us. And I really don't miss seeing Mommy cry. I'm kinda glad we're here."

Cameron looks at me curiously. "I thought you hated this place," he says.

"I thought I did, but it's not so bad," I admit. "While Mom and Dad figure things out, we'll just have to keep having fun and pray that everything's going to be okay."

"Are they going to leave us here?" Cameron cries.

"I don't think so," I say. "Look." I stare into his eyes. "I don't know what'll happen when we get back home, but while we're here let's try not to get down about it. We'll just have to wait to hear what Mom and Dad decide." For Cameron, marriage is all too much to understand. It is for me too, but I have to be strong, at least for him. If our parents do split up, I don't know what will happen to us. Will we have to yo-yo between two places? I have friends who live this way, and most of them hate it. Will we have to meet Daddy's girlfriend? Will Mommy find someone new? *Ugh! I don't even want to think of that happening.* I wipe away falling tears from my little brother's eyes and hug him.

"Stop crying," I demand. "You're a big boy now."

"I'm only seven!" Cameron sobs. "And now we're going to be homeless."

"No, we're not. Mommy and Daddy will not ever let that happen," I say as I look at him. "I know this is scary for you. But me and you, we're going to be okay, all right?" He stares at me with puppy dog eyes, then nods, and I almost forget he's a pain in my butt half the time. "Now, if you don't stop crying, Aunt Jeanie is going to start calling you Captain Cry-a-Lot like she used to do to me when I was little." Cameron smiles. "Remember what I said: let's not worry, and just make the best of the time we have here, okay?"

"Okay, Captain Cry-a-Lot," Cameron cracks. And he's back.

"Ha ha, very funny." I smirk as I shove him out the door. I dash to the window to see if Sally and Uncle Larry are still talking. The last I heard was Uncle Larry telling

Sally that the pool should be ready soon, in enough time for her to have a victory pool party when we win the double Dutch contest. Sally waves off her dad's confidence. At this rate, our team will really need to work hard if we're going to have a shot at the competition.

Country Swag

Just when I think my new team and I are going to pick up where we left off yesterday, the camp has other ideas. On Fridays, they make us spend the whole day learning a bunch of warm-up routines and playing silly games just for fun. I guess this is what the double Dutch coach meant by "group activities." We stretch and do group exercises, and later we'll do potato sack races and two-legged relays with other kids we don't even know. *Weird.* It's supposedly their way of teaching us "how to adjust to others' strengths and weaknesses and still win." It's cool to be grilled about the importance of respect and working together, but what's not cool is the counselors yelling at us like we're some juvenile delinquents at a boot camp. Then again, some of the kids are acting out.

Although a few of the concentration exercises, like carrying an egg on a paper plate as fast as we can for ten yards, make us look like fools, it's fun. At the obstacle course, I'm running next to a boy with long sandy-blond hair. With just one look, we take each other on as competitors. He beats me over the wall, but I pass him as we jump through the tires and cross the finish line first. *Yes!* As we try to catch our breath, we share a laugh and he actually high-fives me. *Nice!*

It feels good to be treated like an athlete—like double Dutch is considered a real sport at this camp. In Brooklyn, jumping double Dutch is "cute" or just a favorite pastime, but here it's a competition like all the others, and double Dutchers are to be reckoned with. *That's pretty cool.* It would be even cooler if I wasn't so nervous about only having two and a half days to practice with my new team. I wonder if messing around with the boys yesterday was worth it. Maybe so, because the whole time, I keep wondering, *Where is Charlie?* I've kept my eyes peeled all morning, but I don't see him anywhere. In the gym, around the water fountain, or at the skateboard park . . . *Okay, am I stalking him?* Maybe he has a girlfriend and he's somewhere with her. Maybe he's sick. Maybe he got hit by a car. *Yeah, I'm losing it.* Then I remember my cousin did say she thinks he likes me. I stare into space, just thinking about his face so close to mine.

"Kayla!" Sally snaps her fingers in my face. "Earth to Kayla."

"What?" I come to.

"It's lunchtime!"

"Oh, okay!" I try to play off my daydream. "So what now?"

Sally shakes her head and runs off to the picnic area.

After Sally and I grab lunch trays, we look around for Melissa and Tina. We spot them sitting in the grass under a tree.

"Why are you guys sitting in the dirt?" I ask. "There are creepy-crawly things down there." *City girl here. Dogs poop in grass.*

"Well, aren't you the queen of England," Melissa snarls with her mouth full of bologna sandwich. "There weren't any more tables."

"We sit in the grass all the time," Tina chimes in. "It's no big deal."

I grab my sandwich off the tray and eat standing up. Sally just rolls her eyes and gracefully lowers, sitting with her legs crossed.

"And I thought *she* was the princess," Melissa says, her mouth again full of food. Sally shoots her a look. "Sorry, but I did," Melissa admits.

I stand a little while longer, not just because I don't want to sit on the grass but because I am still keeping an eye out for the cutest boy I've ever met in my life. *Where can he be?* After realizing Charlie probably didn't come to camp today, I plop down and join my team on the grass. It's not so bad. *Me. Grass. North Carolina. Hmm.* What if my parents left us here? Would I be okay with this? I don't know, but okay, it's not half bad.

"Look! Ants!" a squeaky voice says.

"Where?" I quickly jump back to my feet, shaking and dusting off any possible ants, but there isn't anything except juice dripping from my face. *Ugh!* All I hear is laughter. It's the Bouncing Belles.

"The Brooklyn girl is afraid of bugs! Ha ha!" Ivy laughs.

"Yeah, I am really tired of a certain little bug with beady blue eyes." I charge toward Ivy as I wipe juice from my face. Melissa holds me back.

"So *this* is your crew?" Ivy laughs to the other Belles.

"Yeah, you got something to say about it?" My Brooklyn attitude flares.

"First, you have a loser on your team," Ivy says, referring

to Sally. "Then a bunch of nobodies who probably can't even skip single rope, much less jump double Dutch."

"You might as well quit now," the taller girl says. The Belles agree and snicker. Oooh—I wonder if she's had lunch yet, because I sure do want to feed this girl a knuckle sandwich right now . . . but I can't! I won't let myself go there. If I get in any kind of trouble, that would not be good. *Uuuggghh!* I smirk, the way a superhero smirks before spitting fire or something awesome to crush an enemy.

"First, back up," I say. She doesn't. "Okay then." I get closer and cross my arms to let her know she doesn't scare me. "Second, my cousin is nobody's loser." I glance at Sally, but she cowers. The double Dutch divas grumble. "You just better get ready because this team—yes, this team—is going to ring your little Belles right out of the gym." I think I put more stank on my confidence than I truly have for my team 'cause I'm not about to back down.

Then Ivy stands on her tippy-toes and looks right into my eyes. "Huh" is all she says. Suddenly the rest of her crew busts out laughing.

"Let's go, Ivy," the taller blond Belle calls. "We shouldn't be wasting our time. They don't even have a coach."

"You're right, Brie," Ivy responds. "Why are we wasting our time?" They gather and saunter off like they know they've got us beat already. *This sucks!* That friggin' runt is really getting under my skin, and there's nothing I can do about it but beat them at the competition. I turn to my team.

"Since we won't get any practice today, we'll have to start over the weekend," I say seriously. "Sally's house. Seven a.m."

"Seven?" Melissa grunts.

"But tomorrow is Saturday." Tina isn't happy either.

"Do you guys want to have a chance, or are you going to let those double Dutch bullies keep pouncing on us? Not me," I say, then wait for an answer. But there is none. Until . . . Sally stands.

"I'm ready," she says with determination in her voice. Suddenly I am *so* proud of her.

"Who else?" I try to keep the momentum.

"You're right. I want to crush those heffas!" Melissa shouts. We all turn to Tina.

"Okay." Tina shrugs. "See you guys in the morning." *She's odd.* At this point I don't care if she and Melissa have two left feet. Tomorrow they are going to learn how to double Dutch if we have to stay up all night. I just pray they're fast learners.

Double Trouble

The next morning I am still so on fire from our little run-in with the divas that I don't even eat breakfast. I grab my cousin Marc's old boom box from his dresser and head outside to the driveway. We won't need music for freestyle, but it might help us with our rhythm. Sally actually beats me there.

"Good morning," Sally says as she tightens the laces on her sneakers. Who wears pink BeDazzled sneakers? *My princess cousin, of course.*

"Hey," I reply, surprised. I think my cousin is really starting to show some signs of something, but I'm not sure if it's determination to get back at the girls who have been dragging her through the mud for too long or if she's excited about hanging up her ballet slippers for a minute to do double Dutch again. Either way, it's a side of her I am really happy to see.

Tina and Melissa show up with their long hair tied in ponytails and their game faces on.

"I took this from my backyard just in case," Melissa says, showing me an extra rope. "My mother is going to have a fit when she finds out I took her clothesline."

"People still use those?" I ask.

"Yeah, the people who live in the trailer park," Sally says nonchalantly.

"Got a problem with that, Princess?" Melissa grunts.

"No! I'm just saying." Sally shrugs it off.

"She didn't mean anything," I reassure Melissa. "Let's just get to work."

"Well, *buenos dias,* bitches," Tina says sarcastically. *Did she just call us "bitches"?* As much as I've heard girls around my block call each other names like that, it's just never felt right to me. My mother and father never call me out my name, so no one else should, and before I can say anything, Sally nips it in the bud.

"Tina! Do you guys want my mother to come out here and send you home?" Sally says quietly.

"For what, saying 'bitch'?" Melissa chuckles. "Well, I'm glad I washed my mouth out with soap this morning. I almost forgot we were going to be among royalty." Tina and Melissa share a laugh. I am beginning to think we might have to set a few rules, but I can't think of anything more than not referring to each other as bitches and trailer park people or fake royalty. But judging by our culture clash, something is bound to come up.

Double Dutch might look crazy complicated, but it's not. It's just all the fancy moves and tricks that make it look harder than it really is. Add perfection to it and that's where the competition and fun come in. I want to create complicated moves like those aerial spins between the ropes without making one mistake. But for anyone trying to actually jump double Dutch for the first time, like Tina and Melissa, the hardest part is getting *in* the ropes.

"Ready?" I ask as Sally and I turn the ropes inward, one after another, very slowly, slow enough for a turtle to get in. Melissa stands next to Sally and lunges toward the ropes over and over again as they pass by.

"Come on!" Tina says impatiently. "Jump in already!"

"Quit it, Tina!" Melissa yells back. "You're making me lose my concentration."

"We're turning as slow as we can," Sally says.

"Come on, Melissa, you can do it," I encourage her. "I'll give you a 'go' every time it's good to go in, okay?"

"I got this," Melissa says, determined.

"Okay," I say resignedly. "But remember, jump in with the foot closest to the rope, and then pick up your foot before the rope gets to it. You can do it." Melissa rocks back and forth and back and forth . . . and back and forth. Sally gets frustrated and drops the ropes.

"She's not going to jump!" Sally says.

"Give her a chance!" I yell at Sally. "She'll do it."

"This is useless! She probably doesn't have any rhythm!"

"What do you mean no rhythm?" Melissa shouts at Sally. "Oh, I've got rhythm. Let me hold your iPod, Tina." Tina hands the tiny device to Melissa, who shoves in the earbuds. I love that Melissa is uninhibited about everything, but I am afraid of what is to follow. White girls are not known for their street dancing. Suddenly Melissa is pop-locking! *OMG!* Well, in *my* face! She's killing it and talking like we can't hear her. "I don't have rhythm. . . ." Pop . . . Move . . . Lock . . . Wiggle . . . Pop . . . "Yeah right. This isn't rhythm." I try to contain my joy and laughter. Everything I've thought about white girls and dancing has just been shattered. Go, Melissa!

"Okay, okay!" Sally says. "I get it! You can dance!"

"All right, then, let me jump," Melissa says as we pick up the ropes, with more excitement this time. "One-two-three." Melissa slips into the ropes and kicks her knees up like she's exercising, but she's keeping them off the ropes. "I'm doing it! I'm double-Dutching! Ha ha!"

"Yeah! Keep going! You got it! Awesome!" Sally and I cheer simultaneously. She jumps a few more seconds, then tries to do a turn, but her feet get caught in the ropes. She's done.

"Damn!" Melissa yells. "I mean, darn!"

"You'll have to get the basics before doing other stuff," I tell her. "But that was good!" Melissa jumps up and down, smiling.

"Your turn, Tina," Melissa prompts. "Let's see how you do, Ms. Fancy-Pants."

"Okay." Tina shrugs. Sally and I begin turning the ropes at the same slow pace we did for Melissa.

"Uh, can you guys turn a little faster? Oh, and wait." Tina plugs in her earbuds. Sally and I look at each other like, *What?* We turn faster, as she requested. To our surprise Tina gets in after the third loop! She's jumping and turning and even shaking her head as if she's dancing.

"Tina!" Sally says. "She got it!"

"Wow!" I am in shock.

"Show-off!" Melissa snickers. Tina can't hear a word we're saying with her earbuds in, but she catches the ropes with her feet.

"Huh?" Tina asks.

"That was so awesome, Tina!" Sally says.

"I thought you said you didn't know how to jump," I say.

"Well, I watched some videos online and practiced the footwork in my room," Tina says nonchalantly. "It seems like it's all about rhythm and coordination of the ropes." *Okay.*

"Maybe I'll just be a turner?" Melissa suggests.

"That might be a good idea," Sally agrees. I shoot her a look. "I mean, we'll see."

"Once we get the basics down, we can put in some real moves," I say, picking up the ropes. "So let's keep going until everyone learns each other's rhythm. Everybody needs to be able to jump in at any time, just in case something happens."

"Like what?" Sally crosses her arms. "Like someone freezes?"

"I wasn't even thinking that." I really wasn't. I was thinking a twisted ankle or something like that. Obviously Sally still has jitters about getting back in competition. Now that she's brought it up, I start to think, *What if she does freeze?*

"I'm not going to freeze!" Sally insists. Melissa grabs the other end of the ropes and hands them to Sally.

"Come on, Princess, just in case," Melissa says. "Let me try it again."

"Okay, but stop calling me Princess," Sally says.

"Well, stop treating me like I'm a peasant, and we're good," Melissa answers. Now we're getting along . . . somewhat.

I don't think Melissa is trying to be snide; she is just determined to learn how to jump double Dutch. And as we practice all morning and afternoon, I begin to really like her and Tina. Melissa is gritty and fearless. I admire that about her. She is still struggling with jumping, but I take her to a tree at the end of the yard and wrap the rope around it.

"What are you doing?" Melissa asks.

"This is how almost everyone learns how to turn rope," I say as I try to explain nicely. "The ropes should sound like *tic-tic, tic-tic,* and not *tic—toc, tic—toc.*" I demonstrate. "If it sounds like this, you get called double-handed, which means you can't turn."

"Give me that." Melissa grabs the ends and starts to turn. "Tic-tic, tic-tic," she begins. It's awkward, but she keeps trying to catch the rhythm.

"Keep turning!" I say. "Loosen your arms. You'll get it!"

"All right already!" Melissa yells, irritated. "Let me concentrate."

Melissa doesn't seem like the kind of girl who is easily bossed around, so I leave her alone quickly. She's really getting the rhythm of the ropes now. Tina, on the other hand . . . Her dancing skills are turning out to be really helpful, but we'll have to get her to jump without earbuds so she can hear us. We can't have those earbuds getting in the way of the ropes. That's going to be a challenge.

Although we spend all day together getting the basics down, we haven't even come close to putting together a routine. We still have work ahead of us if we're going to compete like a real team, or even possibly be able to beat those Belles. Melissa trips and falls. *Ugh!* Looks like tomorrow is going to be another full day of double Dutch.

Now that Tina and Melissa know how to get *in* the ropes and jump for a few beats, Sally and I spend Sunday teaching them the first test in double Dutch: compulsory, where our teammates turn the ropes like a slow-speed eggbeater while the other two jumpers lift the left leg over the right and then right over left, careful not to catch or stop the ropes. *No biggie, right? Well . . .* Sally and I turn really slow and count them in: "Ready? One-two-three-four-*go!*" we call. First Tina gets in, then Melissa. *Good!* But they soon mess up. *No!*

"I'm sorry!" Melissa apologizes. "One more time, one more time!"

If they don't get this, we'll never qualify. I don't want us to fail. I try not to worry and we start all over again . . . and again, and again. We keep going until the sprinklers and the house lights come on. Finally they get the compulsory down pat. And we haven't even begun to think of a routine. I guess we'll have to do that at camp . . . in front of everybody.

It took us all weekend long, but I'm glad Sally and I were able to teach Melissa and Tina the basics of double Dutch. *Thank goodness!* Hmm, I never thought my cousin and I would work *together* on anything. Now, at camp, as the teams are called, we'll have to show the coaches what we can do. There are two younger teams, ten-year-olds who are so cute with their game faces on. They're pretty good with their leapfrog and push-up routines. Even though it's baby stuff, Tina's and Melissa's mouths are open in awe. The other older team is the Belles. They try to show off some of their freestyle with a few double-handed flips and cartwheels, a more toned-down version of what Sally and I saw a few days ago, but it's good. *Okay, really good.* It's our turn. The Belles snicker as we take the floor.

"Let's not try anything fancy," I tell my team. They're obviously nervous.

"We can't," Melissa blurts out. "I don't know half the things those little kids did."

"We'll just do what we learned," I say reassuringly. "Compulsory."

"This is not cool." Sally ducks her head. I know it's not crushing the Belles, but we have to show them we can at *least* jump.

Very carefully and slowly, Melissa and Sally jump in . . . and lift one foot . . . and out. All I keep thinking is *Don't mess up! Get it right!* One down. Then Tina and I do the same. Yes, we did it! We hear a little snicker, probably from the Belles, but hey, no one said we *had* to do a whole routine, so we leave it at that.

"Uh, okay. Good, you guys," says Coach Kirsten. "So are you planning on competing in speed and freestyle as well, or . . . ?"

"Yes." "No." "Freestyle?" "What's that?" The four of us speak at once. I shoot my team a look, then step up as if I am captain.

"Yes, we'll be competing in speed and freestyle," I say matter-of-factly. I'm faking it, but I can't bring myself to chicken out.

"Oh, come on! They're not ready for speed," Ivy heckles. "They can barely jump."

I give her a hard stare. She just had to push me.

"Can you turn?" I ask the blond coach, which catches her off guard.

"Uh, yeah, sure," she says as she grabs the ropes from my hands. I hand the other end to Sally.

"Just keep your eye on my left foot like your life depends on it," I say, looking directly into Sally's eyes.

"Left foot. Right. Okay." Sally doesn't flinch. As the ropes begin to spin, a silence comes over the gym. All eyes are on me. I get in the ropes and . . . my foot gets caught! *Ugh!* There's laughter, and I can imagine from who.

"Give her a chance." The coach quiets the group. I quickly think about why I'm here and how my cousin is looking at me like a big sister now. I must get this right. I glide through the ropes and find a groove.

"One-two, one-two! Faster!" I yell as I focus on Sally's hands. They turn faster and the ropes sound like wind in a storm as they spin around my head. I keep jumping through the *ooh*s and *aah*s! I stay focused until I feel like I've given them enough. The jumpers applaud as I slow down and jump out with ease. Everyone's impressed except for the Belles. They smirk as if to say, *So what?* Who cares? That wasn't even my best.

"That's *my* teammate. Whoop-whoop!" Melissa and Tina cheer.

"Wow! That was great!" Coach Kirsten says, impressed. "I think we have a real competitor here." I smile at my cousin, who is relieved we were able to show them we have more than they think we have. The coach hands me the ropes, then turns to the entire group. "Okay, jumpers, we have only a couple more weeks before regionals."

"Two weeks?" I scream, shocked.

"Yeah, right, they'll be ready for regionals!" Ivy calls out sarcastically as everyone laughs.

"Quiet down, everyone," Coach Kirsten commands. She is no Ms. Jackson, who would have been blowing the heck out of her whistle. Coach Kirsten turns her attention back to our hodgepodge team. "I think you guys might be able to compete in speed, but your numbers have to be really impressive for nationals." She has no idea how good I *really* am at speed. "And if you want to go for freestyle, well, you'll have to put a routine together pretty quickly. Do you think you can do that?"

"Yes." "No?" "Maybe." Again, clearly we're not on the same page.

"We'll be ready," I say, faking confidence.

"Okay, good," she says, "I look forward to seeing it." She's being nice, but I don't think she believes we can do it. She turns to the group. "And that goes for everyone. We'll help you with compulsory if you need it, and speed. If you're competing in freestyle, which three teams are, remember you'll have to come up with your own two-minute routine. The coaches are only here to supervise freestyle. So you and your team captain will have to decide on everything. Music, costumes . . ."

Two weeks keeps ringing in my head! It was hard enough teaching Melissa and Sally compulsory. Now a whole routine in two weeks!

"Kayla, we can't come up with a routine in two weeks," Sally practically cries. "What are we gonna do?"

"We can't quit," I say. "Quitters are losers."

"I'm no loser!" Melissa exclaims.

"Let's rock!" Tina adds. Sally takes a big breath as I grab her hand.

"Come on," I encourage them. "We've got work to do!"

Love-Struck

It's a week before the regional competitions and we're *still* at the camp practicing. Every morning I look around to see if I can spot Charlie, but I don't. I begin to think he left or maybe I just keep missing him. Then again, Sally and I have been so focused that all we do is head straight to the gym and hit the floor with Tina and Melissa. We're learning our strengths and weaknesses. Melissa is an awkward jumper, but now she's a strong turner. Tina is, well, she's rhythmic but still jumps with her earbuds. I guess since she lives with younger siblings, she might be in the habit of tuning people out like I do at my house just so I can do homework. Or maybe it's her way of getting focused. Whatever the reason, the earbuds or anything that could catch the ropes makes me nervous. She's got to be able to hear us when she's jumping. I don't know how, but we're going to have to get her to jump without them. Either way, Tina's cool and she's doing really good.

We're going over some of the simpler tricks, like pop-ups, push-up jumps, cartwheel entries, and hopefully a flip if we can even try it. Demonstrating to Melissa and Tina isn't hard; it's getting them to not be afraid to get hit by the ropes, which happens a lot, that is. One thing is for sure: we're not getting much attention from the coaches, especially Kirsten. We'll get a "Keep it up, girls!" from one or two of them, but that's it. They're not hounding us like Ms. Jackson and her crew back in Brooklyn would, but some help would be great. I think the coaches are putting all their hopes on the Belles. Well, we'll see about that.

But the only way we're going to beat those double Dutch divas, the Belles, is if we put together a crazy freestyle routine that no one can touch. And if it takes all weekend to start putting something together . . . *Hmm . . . I don't know.* And as much as I hate to admit it, the Belles are really good. But there's no time for doubt; we have to just get to it. Right when I think we can finally move on, the counselors call us together after lunch.

"Okay, everybody!" A redheaded counselor runs through

the gym doors and shouts into a bullhorn. "Today we're giving you guys a break." *Really? We can't stop now!* A nerdy guy counselor takes the stage and looks around at everyone.

"In the words of Muhammad Ali," he says, " 'I hated every minute of training, but I said, Don't quit. Suffer now and live the rest of your life as a champion.' "

"But no rest is worth anything except the rest that is earned," the redhead adds. "And you guys have worked hard and earned a day of fun!"

"So for the rest of the day . . . wait for it, wait for it," the nerdy counselor jokes. "You guys will have arts and crafts!"

Everyone looks around and chuckles at each other like, *What? Seriously? Do we look like babies to them?* We don't have time for arts and crafts. We've got a double Dutch routine we have to put together. While everyone clamors over the counselors' orders, I get an idea.

"Hey, guys," I say as I stand and face Sally, Tina, and Melissa. "Why don't we leave and practice at Sally's?" They give me this look like I've gotten on their last nerve.

"Slave-drive much?" groans Tina.

I guess they're right. Maybe the time off will be good for everybody who's ready, but we aren't. I sulk as our coaches gather the double Dutch teams to follow the other teams across the courtyard into the cafeteria. Sally nudges me.

"Look!" Sally directs her focus to the other side of the courtyard. It's Charlie! *He's back!* I haven't seen him since our football game in the park. Where has he been? Was he sick? Was he hiding from me? Was I stalking much? Oh my God! He catches me staring. I look around toward the sky like a bee is buzzing near me. I swat imaginary bees. Okay, it's a stupid thing to do, but I have to play it off. I glance again to see if he saw my terrible acting. He did. But he's smiling. Is he laughing at me or was that a *smile* smile? And now there it goes again. My heart is fluttering. *What is that?* I have to get a grip. *He's just a boy! A really cute one, but just be cool.* Maybe arts and crafts is exactly what I need to calm down these darn butterflies in my stomach.

"I told you he likes you." Sally smirks. I can't help but let this stupid grin grow on my face. *Me?* I never knew boys like him really existed, or maybe I just wasn't that interested until now. Melissa and Tina have been watching the whole thing.

"Kayla's got a crush," teases Melissa. "Kayla's got a cru-ush."

"Kayla's got a cru-ush," Tina chimes in. Now it's a song. *Ugh! Is this necessary?* Sally crosses her arms as if something is bothering her.

The counselors order us into lines like we are first graders, then lead us to the cafeteria. Crepe paper, construction paper, streamers, markers, chalk, every watercolor you can think of, crayons, glue, even feathers and other stuff, is on every long lunch table. It looks like a preschool threw up in there, but in a nice way, and judging by the cheers and excitement, everyone is suddenly okay being a kid again.

"All right," the redhead announces. "Sit wherever you like, and enjoy!"

Music blares through the speakers and we dig into all the fun stuff awaiting us. I don't know if he did this on purpose, but Charlie and his skateboard-football friends sit directly across the table from us. Sally and Melissa look at me like they smell something fishy. Tina couldn't care less. She's already busy making stick figures with fuzzy wire. Melissa clears her throat and leans over to me and Sally.

"There's something up their sleeve," she whispers, then gives one of the smaller boys an evil eye. He looks around nervously.

"Maybe we should move somewhere else," suggests Sally loudly.

"Don't go," Charlie says. "We don't bite. Right, Tommy?"

"But somebody on your team does." Tommy grimaces. "See, I have teeth marks right here." He lifts his arm. Melissa smirks.

"You should get that checked," a short kid with glasses says as he examines Tommy's arm.

"Knock it off, Tim!" barks Tommy. Tim flinches as Sally covers her mouth to keep from laughing out loud.

"We were here first," I say, staring right into Charlie's eyes. "So we're definitely staying." I don't know if I'm accepting another challenge or learning to tame the butterflies in my stomach. Either way, I feel challenged.

"Okay then," Sally says as she bashfully looks away from Charlie. "Let's make art, shall we?" If I didn't know any better, I would think my cousin had a crush on Charlie too. It's just that way she looks at him. *Hmm.*

Without taking our eyes off one another, we each grab a utensil of our choice: a marker, paintbrush, crayon, paper, watercolors, a small cup of water, whatever we want. I try to concentrate, but I am curious to see what Charlie is drawing. He scoots around as if I'm cheating off his test. I turn my attention back to my work. It's quiet for a while, but the tension seems so loud. It's like I am talking to Charlie, but without saying a word. He seems so confident. Maybe that's why I like him. There, I admit it. *I like Charlie!*

"Look what I'm drawing," Tommy says as he holds up his artwork. "It's a sketch of the woman who bit me. I'm going to take it to the police." The picture is an exaggeration of a girl with a big mouth and teeth biting the arm of a smaller boy with a football in his hand. The messy drawing oddly resembles Melissa. We all laugh.

"I think he just called you a woman," Tina whispers to Melissa.

"I don't know what you're talking about." Melissa grimaces. "I am no woman."

"He's flirting with you, stupid!" Tina smacks her forehead in disbelief. Melissa has an uncomfortable look on her face like she's holding in a fart or something. I guess no one's ever flirted with her, and she doesn't know what to do with the information.

"Well, look what I painted," I interrupt. It's a watercolor of a football. "Oh, but I'm not done yet. I'm going to fill in the lines with pink glitter because my cousin made the touchdown and she deserves a trophy. Don't you think it's nice?" Sarcastically, I look at my friends. They all agree. They like it and nod.

"I made a flower," Tim says as he looks at Sally bashfully. Charlie and Tommy are embarrassed for him. Sally gives him her infamous *Seriously?* look.

Tina hands a blue fuzzy wire flower to the kid she dusted at the park. "I'm sorry I tricked you the other day, but next time don't be such a sucker."

"Uh, okay?" The boy doesn't know what to think of the backhanded gesture, but he takes the flower anyway. Tina turns quickly, whipping her ponytail in his face. His cheeks turn beet red. Looks like he's got a crush on Tina.

"Well, I'm going to need more water for my masterpiece,"

Charlie says, which piques my interest. *What is he making?* "Come on, Tommy. I'm going to need your help." They grab cups from the table and leave. Sally and I look at each other and shrug. I have no idea what he's up to, so I get back to my glitter and glue.

Melissa leans over again. "I know they're up to something." She looks at Tim, who acts like he's not listening. He glances up at someone behind us, and before we can turn around, water is pouring down our backs.

Oh my gosh! I can't believe he did that!

Of course I grab the cup I've been cleaning my paintbrush in and hold it for a second while I think.

"I dare ya," taunts Charlie.

I think for a moment. . . . Should I? *Yes!*

I toss the water, but he ducks and it hits some random boy in the back of the head. When the boy turns around, I point to Charlie. By this time the whole camp is watching. Well, everyone except the counselors, who've left us unsupervised for no apparent reason. The tall boy rises slowly and grabs a roll of red streamer, then squeezes glue onto the outside of it. As if in slow motion, he throws it and we both duck. The gluey streamer hits a girl with long blond hair and sticks to her forehead while the roll falls to the ground. She looks like she's bleeding red streamer. She is flabbergasted! Within two seconds, the room erupts into all-out warfare with art supplies.

I smash Charlie in the face with glue and feathers. He smears pink paint all over my face. *He touched my face!* There's so much stuff flying everywhere it is hard to see. Suddenly a long whistle sounds. *Uh-oh!*

Luckily it's the end of the day, and thankfully Sally and I rode bikes this time. Uncle Larry would never let us in the backseat of his car unless he was able to somehow hose us down. We look like we've just been in a food fight, only more sparkly, with paint and feathers glued in our hair like we're punk rockers.

"Well, I'm glad no one told on us," says Tina as feathers fly out of her mouth.

"Yeah, we would've been in a crapload of trouble if they called our parents," Melissa agrees.

I'm happy too, especially because I saw Charlie again. If he likes me, he sure is showing it in the weird way my dad warned me about. He might be confident, but not confident enough to say what he's feeling. *Boys!*

"Kayla!" Sally yells at me. "Are you still in a daze over Charlie? 'Cause we have to figure out what we're going to do about double Dutch practice." Right! How could I forget?

"Um, yeah." I'm back. "No, I am thinking about the competition." *Freestyle!* I freak out in my head because

I don't want to freak out in front of them. "We have to figure out our freestyle. Let's start bright and early tomorrow. We'll have to choreograph a perfect and flawless routine."

"I'll say," Tina chimes in. "Those Belles left after they announced we were going to 'relax and do art.'"

"They probably snuck out way before that," Melissa adds. "'Cause I sure was looking to give the little double Dutch divas a fistful of feathers."

"That means they are really going to bring it," confirms Sally.

"Well, we'll have to work even harder," I say, determined. "I didn't come this far to lose to some country bumpkins. No offense."

"None taken," the three of them respond.

"Okay. Tomorrow. Seven a.m., Sally's," I say. I put my hand out. "Come on, don't leave me hanging." They look at my sticky, feathered, glittery hand for a moment, then one by one they throw in their equally messed-up hands. "Bring it, on three. One-two-three!"

"Bring it!" We all reach our hands up as feathers fly everywhere; we swat them away and laugh. Things may be funny now, but the pressure is on. We've got to have a good practice or we're doomed.

Step It Up

The next morning, Melissa and Tina show up to work on our routine, but for the first two hours we get compulsory down to a science. This time Melissa and I turn first while Sally and Tina jump, then we switch. We want to make sure this doesn't mess up our chances to compete in speed and freestyle. Hopefully we get that far. So it's better to be safe than sorry and make sure we can do compulsory with perfection. A thousand times, done and done. But after that, we can't seem to get anything right. *Ugh! This is not working AT ALL!* Compulsory is one thing, but freestyle is a whole other beast. In order for us to even be competitive, we have to show our skills by doing tricks, or whatever else we can to wow the crowd, within the ropes for one minute. And on top of that, we have to do it flawlessly. No mistakes, no stopping the ropes, and we have to look good. Right now we look horrible.

"No!" I yell at Tina as I almost pull my braids out. "You have to wait until I exit the rope, then you come in."

"Okay, I'm sorry. I got confused," Tina sighs. "I thought you said jump in behind you and then you'll exit."

"I'm sorry," I say. "I mean, it's good that you're trying, but we're really not getting anywhere."

"Can we take a break?" Melissa asks. "My arms are tired."

"We're never going to win," says Sally. "The Belles are going to beat us. I know it!"

"Please! Stop being so negative!" I say with frustration in my voice. "It's bad enough we're having a hard time. Being negative doesn't help."

"I'm just saying, we've been practicing all morning and we can't get one thing right," continues Sally.

Ugh! Ugh! And ugh! She can really kill a spirit good and dead. I stare at her in disgust and turn away. That's just the type of attitude that stops everything. Unfortunately this is one thing about my cousin I've noticed since we were little. When she's having fun, things are great, but when things don't go the way she hopes, she hops on the negative train all the way to Miseryville. I hope she'll grow out of that. I heard my dad say one time that "being negative never won a championship." And right now I completely understand what he means.

In seconds there's a car in the driveway. It's my cousin Marc, Sally's older brother.

"Hey, what y'all doing out here in the hot sun?" Marc yells from the car window as he pulls up. "Hey now, is that my li'l cuz MaKayla from BK, New York City?" I wave to him with a giggle. I haven't seen him since I was seven. I almost forgot how he looked, but he's definitely taller and has a lot more muscles. "Ladies," he says to Tina and Melissa. "Hey, sista Sally from the valley." Sally rolls her eyes at her silly brother. Marc seems so cool and upbeat all the time. Like he never has a bad day and always finds something to laugh about. He hops out of the car and rushes to the other side to open the door. A girl gets out—his girlfriend, I assume.

"Everyone, this is Gabriella," Marc says proudly as he carefully watches every move of her skirt. It's obvious. He's in love. Gabriella glances over at us like we're germs but waves politely. Maybe she's just one of those stuck-up college girls who forgot what it's like to be a kid.

Marc runs over to Sally and gives her a big bear hug,

which obviously makes her uncomfortable. "Put me down!" Sally fights his affection. "You smell like a whole bottle of cologne!"

"Is that right? Well, the grown ladies love it," he kids. Then he turns to me.

"Kayla, girl." Marc stares at me with a smile. "Look at you. You're just as pretty as Aunt Sarah! Come here and give me a hug." Really! That's the same thing my aunt said. Maybe they mean it and it's true . . . or is it just more *Southern hospitality*?

Suddenly my little cousins Michael and Eddie burst through the door, followed by Cameron. They jump on Marc, toppling him to the lawn. Aunt Jeanie and Uncle Larry appear soon after like a welcoming committee. Uncle Larry greets his son as if he hasn't seen him since forever, and Aunt Jeanie gives the girlfriend a stiff smile. It's hard for Aunt Jeanie to fake her feelings. But maybe she just doesn't know much about the girl and doesn't trust that Gabriella's not going to break her firstborn's heart. I've seen it all too many times in the movies.

Marc and his girlfriend head inside as we try to pick up where we left off.

"Why don't we just admit it: we're not going to win," Sally insists. *And we're back to negative again.*

"We're not giving up," Melissa chimes in. "We'll just have to think of something."

"Thank you, Melissa," I say. "I'm glad someone's staying positive."

"How about trying something with music first?" Tina suggests.

"That's a good idea!" I say, reinvigorated. Until:

"Hey, girls," calls Aunt Jeanie from the stoop. "Why don't you ladies come in for some lunch and visit with Marc for a while?" She had the team at *Hey, girls.* I drop the ropes and join everyone inside. Okay, maybe we are doomed. *Ugh!* Sally's negativity is becoming contagious. *I can't let that happen.* I decide to just forget it for now and have lunch.

Aunt Jeanie gathers everyone in the family room to eat. Marc wants us to watch some video of him and his frat brothers. Tina and Melissa are looking around like they have no idea what to expect, and neither do I. He casts a video from his phone to the TV. It's a step contest! And it's crazy!

"A step contest?" Tina asks, genuinely confused. "What's stepping?"

"It's kind of like synchronized dancing," Melissa answers. "It's an African thing." Everyone stares at Melissa for a moment. It's awkward. "What? My cousin dates a black guy from Morehouse," she says with a little Egyptian move, as if it clears the air. I snicker. I can't help it. She is so funny.

"Well, you're sort of right, Melissa," says Marc's girl-friend. "Fraternities and sororities at all colleges put on some sort of display of discipline and organization. And at some black colleges, yes, we step."

"And we Q's are off the chain!" Marc says. "Ain't that right, Gabriella?"

"You guys are a'ight," Gabriella kids. My uncle clears his throat, to which she says, "Okay, you guys *are* the best."

"That's more like it," Uncle Larry says as he and Marc bump fists. I'm guessing he's from the same fraternity.

"Well, come on here, girls, and check this out," Marc says, directing our attention to the TV screen. "I'ma show y'all what stepping is." All of us sit there and keep our eyes peeled as Marc casts another video. We watch these guys put on a show of chants and stepping routines. There's music and lights, and the moves are strong, with stomps and lots of high energy. The guys get the audience into it. And it works. People are cheering and jumping out of their seats. The family room erupts in applause when Marc's fraternity is done.

"This is great!" says Tina, really into it. "That was so awesome!"

"You were great, Marc!" I say. "You guys make college seem like so much fun."

"It ain't all fun and games, li'l cuz," Marc says with a smile. "Like Gabby said, it's a display of discipline . . .

mixed with a little fun. But, yes, the university experience is pretty awesome."

Aunt Jeanie steps over everyone to plant a kiss on her son's cheek. I wouldn't believe it if she wasn't proud of anything Marc did.

"Good grades *and* talented," says Aunt Jeanie, excited.

"Thanks, Mama, but I don't want to take all the credit," says Marc. "I had a secret weapon." He looks at Gabriella. She seems surprised by what he just said.

"Honey?" says Gabriella. "I am captain of the cheerleading squad," she explains to us, "and I just showed him a few moves is all." *Ah! That's where the snooty air came from: captain of the cheerleading squad.*

"Well, I wouldn't tell *my* frat brothers that," Uncle Larry insists. "As a matter of fact, I'm gonna act like I didn't even hear that. Girls choreographing us back in the day would've never happened." *Wait! I suddenly have an idea.*

"Maybe you can help us with our routine," Melissa says to Gabriella. She beat me to it! *Who cares if Marc's girlfriend is snooty? We'll use all the help we can get.*

"Yeah, would you help us, please?" says Tina.

"Maybe just start us off?" I say with a beggar's face. I never thought I'd have to ask anyone to help me with anything that has to do with double Dutch, but with Melissa and Tina being new to it and Sally's negative attitude, I have no choice.

"Help with what?" asks Gabriella. "What are you guys talking about?" I just grab her hand and lead her outside to the driveway.

"Double Dutch?" She laughs. "Really?" She takes another look at our awkward team.

"Well, me and Kayla have been jumping for years," Sally explains. "But Tina and Melissa are beginners."

"Good beginners, might I add," Melissa chimes in.

"And we're fast learners." Tina smiles big like she's begging too. Gabriella crosses her arms and ponders things a moment. Then:

"Okay, I think I might be able to give you a few pointers." She twists her long locks into a bun and looks back at Marc standing in the door. He waves at her as if to say, *Go ahead.*

"I also used to be captain of my double Dutch team outside of high school," Gabriella boasts. "I might be a little rusty, but let's see what we can do."

It's obvious Gabriella knows what she's doing the minute she picks up the ropes and hands the ends to me and Sally.

"Double Dutch is not just simply jumping rope. It's about teamwork, thinking as one team, one unit. Unity with style and flair," Gabriella explains. "Let's stay here." She points two fingers back and forth between her eyes and ours. "Okay?" Sally and I nod. "Good. Now turn and keep your eyes on my feet." I can't believe it. This girl is going to jump! Isn't she too old for this?

In seconds, Gabriella smoothly jumps in the ropes as Sally and I keep our eyes glued to her feet. She does pop-ups, jumps out and back, in and out through the other side and back again. This time she slows her speed and does a couple of split jumps! Wow! I suddenly have a different respect for her. Anyone who knows and loves double Dutch like I do is my new bestie. I love her! As she jumps out, there's silence.

"That's what I mean about staying here." Gabriella connects our eyes again with her fingers.

"Man, that was awesome!" Melissa says.

"Thank you, sweetie," Gabriella says as she pulls herself back together. "Now it's your turn. Let's see what you've got."

Tina pushes play on the boom box for inspiration. Gabriella and I carefully turn the ropes to show Tina and Melissa what to do while Sally does a trick, jumping on her hands, then flipping into a split jump. *Wow! My li'l cousin is good.* Tina takes my end so Sally and I can jump. Gabriella shows Tina and Melissa how to keep up with the moves as Sally and I try a leapfrog jump and flip, but we catch the ropes.

"Ladies," says Gabriella, getting our attention. "We need to get on the same page."

"I knew it." Sally sulks. "We're not going to be good enough to beat the Belles. It's no use."

"First, you've got to stop with the defeatist attitude," scolds Gabriella. "I don't know one winner who ever doubted themselves." I shoot Sally a look like, *I hope that sank in that head of yours.* "It's only one minute, right? So maybe we should start with your personal strengths. Do you guys have anything special, any other physical skills that you can do individually?"

"I'm in gymnastics, but I love to dance," says Tina. "Salsa, like ballroom salsa."

"I'm a ballerina and I take gymnastics too," says Sally, brightening.

"I jump double Dutch every chance I get," I say confidently.

Melissa's turn. "I just want to smash those b—" I quickly put my finger to my lips, signaling her to stop before she says the B-word. "Okay, I pitch softball and I also like wrestling my brothers. Oh, and I can pop-lock!" Well, at least she's honest. *Respectable.* Gabriella snickers as if she doesn't believe it.

"She can." I encourage Melissa. "Go ahead. Show her." Melissa begins beatboxing with her mouth and dancing.

"Nice!" Gabriella is impressed. Melissa keeps going until Sally stops her.

"She gets it," Sally says. Melissa shoves Sally's hand off her.

"That was great. This is all good to know," says Gabriella. She puts one hand on her hip and scratches her temple. "Okay, let me think." She paces. I am so glad Gabriella is here helping us, because even though we have some good skills it would take us forever to figure out how to work them into our routine. She must be an expert or something, because in seconds, she puts us to work like Mr. Miyagi and the Karate Kid. She charges Melissa with mastering turning, which means she has to practice with a rope wrapped around a tree again, but this time bending her knees up and down. I don't think she likes it, but she's doing it. Tina is in charge of making up the dance routine we can do in the ropes.

"They should be current dance moves. None of that cabbage-patch-running-man stuff," Gabriella says.

"I don't even know what that is, but okay." Tina is on it. Somehow I know there will be salsa dancing in there somewhere.

And as for me and Sally, Gabriella ponders a routine for us.

"I have an idea!" Sally says. "Maybe I can do the

jumping spider? It's the move I was supposed to do when I was with the Belles. Every double Dutch routine that ever got high scores had at least one insane move."

"And so you want to do the move you were afraid to do *and* froze on?" I ask, unconvinced.

"Yes!" Sally replies. "I know I messed up before, but I know I can do it." Gabriella looks at me and I shrug. I figure, if she's ready to show her frenemies she can do the move without them, then I think we should let her do it.

"Okay," Gabriella decides. "Let's try it, and we'll add on any of the best tricks we can come up with from there." Sally and I agree. "We can do this, ladies!" Gabriella gets excited and we all cheer! We all have our work cut out for us, and if the routine focuses on Sally and me being the main jumpers, we just might have a chance.

After about two and half hours, four sweaty towels, and twenty glasses of iced tea, we have a routine. *Yes!* We'll still need to work on it and pull everything together without stopping the ropes, but the groundwork is done. Now keeping Sally's confidence in us as a new team hopefully won't be a challenge. Just as we are ready to get started again, like sneaky creepy-crawlies, the Bouncing Belles roll by on their bikes.

"Look." Melissa calls our attention to them. The Belles have weird smirks on their faces and give fake waves. I'm not feeling their vibe.

"Competition?" Gabriella is suspicious.

"Yeah, they used to be my friends," Sally says somberly. "But now they're just . . . mean."

"Do you think they were watching us? Like, saw our routine?" Tina asks.

"Would they copy us?" Melissa asks.

"I doubt it," Sally answers. "They're too good to steal someone else's routine."

"I don't know," I say. "If they do anything to copy us, I will kick that little one's—"

"You will act like a lady," Gabriella cuts me off. "Competitors compete, not fight. Fighting is for savages. Are you savages or are you tough competitors who just put together an awesome routine and are ready to leave it all on the floor?" We nod. "I can't hear you!" Gabriella screams.

"Yes!" we all scream back.

"All right then, let's do this one more time, with lots of energy this time." Gabriella gets us pumped again. "Hit the music, Tina!"

Tina turns the music on, and we get back into it. Melissa's turning skills are pretty good, but Sally keeps blaming her for stopping the ropes. Those two are making me nervous. Gabriella pays it no mind and makes us practice our routine three more times until we collapse.

• • •

145

Before sunset, Marc and Gabriella say their good-byes. All of us thank Gabriella for her help. I guess she wasn't so snooty after all. I have to stop being so quick to judge people. My mother always tells me that judging a book by its cover is easy to do; be open to the possibility that people might surprise you, she says. *Check.* The car begins to roll out of the driveway but comes to a screeching halt.

"Girls!" yells Gabriella. We all run to the car window. "Remember what I said: double Dutch is about jumping two ropes but one team, as a unit. Oh, and get really cute outfits. It helps with the 'wow' factor." We watch them drive off, then stare at each other.

"Costumes? Oh my God, we forgot about costumes!" We all panic.

"Don't worry, girls," says Aunt Jeanie. "One trip to the mall . . . and I mean one trip. How's that sound?"

We all jump around with excitement. The only thing that can make this moment even better is if we win the double Dutch competition . . . and if I see Charlie again, of course.

Second to None

It's qualification day at the Charlotte Sports Day Camp, and the place is crawling with players and parents from all over the city. As for me and my team, we worked all day on Sunday and it was tough, but we're ready. Melissa learned that if she keeps her eyes on our feet, she'll turn the ropes carefully. Tina worked out a fly dance, and Sally and I got our tricks down pat. I made sure we knew our routine backward and forward. Sally is no longer "frozen" in time and seems to have put the past on ice so she can focus on her new task, beating the Belles. We're all sore, but we look good . . . as good as we can with two new jumpers who really get it. As for me, *I am so ready!*

In the car on the way to camp, Sally seems to be more excited than I am, but I'm skeptical. She's been nervous and very negative about everything except picking out the coolest costumes. I just hope she doesn't let the Belles get in her head again, because she is so good at double Dutch. I can't believe she let those bullies tear down her confidence. Well, they won't today. Not if I can help it. We've practiced too hard. There's no way we can lose.

Uncle Larry and Aunt Jeanie pick up Tina and Melissa so we can show up as a team. Tina has woven ribbons into her two pigtails, then intertwined them on top of her head, which looks really cool. She must have done Melissa's hair too, because she actually looks neat and oddly girlyish. Sally and I have football-black makeup under our eyes, so we all look like we're ready for war. And maybe there is something to showing solidarity, because when we arrive at the gym and Uncle Larry opens the door for us, everyone watches us like we're rock stars. This moment has that "ooow" effect like that scene in a music video when everything slows down. One by one, we step out of the car—first Tina, then Melissa, then Sally, and then me. We stand there for the spectators, straightening our superlight puff jackets that read 4-D in satin and sequins that Aunt Jeanie helped sew on so we'd really look unique. The 4-D stands for "Double Deuces," also known as the peace sign for anyone who tries to defeat us in double Dutch. We pose with the two-finger peace sign as Aunt Jeanie takes our picture. Courage and confidence are a part of any competitive sport, and we have plenty. In unison, we reach into our pockets for our shades and put them on to cover our eyes from the sun . . . and, uh, maybe from the imaginary cameras of the imaginary paparazzi? *Oh yeah, kids are checking our style.* We soak in the attention.

And as if on cue, Charlie and his boys roll by on their skateboards! They nearly fall over themselves checking us out. I keep my cool, although I am doing backflips in my mind. *Perfect timing!* We look their way as we continue walking. Charlie smiles and then winks at me. *What?* As much as I want to stop and catch up since our *artsy* fight, I turn away and keep moving. *I have no time for distractions.* I'm in double Dutch mode.

The gym is filled with double Dutch teams from what seems like all over North Carolina. All I can see is Carolina blue everywhere, on every team's outfits including ours. I guess it's part of the pride here. *Cool.* Parents and kids are in the stands watching. It feels more like a party with a DJ included. Suddenly I have a vision of my parents in the audience, but just as I start to smile from the obvious daydream, a loud whistle snaps me back to reality. And before we take our places, we drop our written program at the judges' table and Sally hustles over to give an extra copy to the DJ just in case.

"This is awesome!" Melissa says excitedly. "I had no idea this was so friggin' popular."

"Me neither," admits Tina. "This is like some underground hip-hop-type stuff. I love it." I look at her peculiarly. What does a Latina know about underground hip-hop? *Isn't that for city kids to know and country kids to find out? I guess she has.*

"I have to go to the bathroom," Sally blurts out.

"You went to the bathroom three times before we left. Are you just nervous?" I ask.

"What if I mess up? What if the Belles laugh at me again?" Sally says.

"Look at me, Sally," I say as I put my hands on her shoulders and look right into her eyes. She looks away. "Look at me!" She does. "You're not going to do anything but go out there and have fun. We've practiced our routine, and even with new double Dutchers on our team, we got this!"

"Yeah, Sally," Melissa says. "Even if we don't win. We're good. But if they laugh at you—or any of us—I'll punch them right in the nose."

"Okay, Melissa." I have to stop her. "There won't be any need for that. We'll do just fine if we stick to the routine."

"But how do you know?" asks Sally.

"Because I know!" I insist. "Look, I never said this to you before, but I think you are incredible at double Dutch, and you're probably an even better ballerina. I couldn't be that graceful if I tried. But once you lock into something you love doing, you are fierce, li'l cuz! Those Belles, those bullies, just caught you on a bad day at that last competition. Maybe you just weren't sure of yourself, I don't know. But today you're even better than before, and I think as a team, we're really good. So stop worrying!"

"That's right! We may be new, but we're good," Tina chimes in. "Sally, sometimes you have to let people know you're a force to be reckoned with! And today, like Gabriella told us, we're working together as one team, one force!" *Yes, go, Tina!*

"One team, one force!" says Melissa as she puts her hand out, expecting us to join in. Sally thinks about it for a second and then stacks her hand on top of Melissa's.

"One team, one force!" exclaims Sally. Tina and I add our hands to the stack.

"Let's show *all* these double Dutch teams 4-D just stepped into the building," I say confidently. "Double Deuces on three! One-two-three!"

"Double Deuces!" we shout.

Here the judges are serious. In New York, the judges

would at least look you in the eye and wish you luck, but not here. Your team has to be ready to turn as soon as they come around. All they say is "Ready? Jump!" And we do. To start, we have to pass the compulsory test. Tina and Melissa turn while Sally and I jump first. We want to show Tina and Melissa how easy it is, and then we can cheer them on as we turn for them. I have confidence they can do it. The plan works. Tina and Melissa do it! *Flawless.* The second test: speed. My specialty. And of course as soon as I get in the ropes, the judges struggle to keep count each time my left foot hits the floor. Thank goodness there are two judges for comparison. They count 333 steps in two minutes. *Yes!* Better than my last record.

There's another whistle. I guess this means break time to clear the stage for freestyle. We all run to the restroom to clear out the jitters and change outfits, and that's when we collide with the Bouncing Belles, aka the double Dutch bullies. They are all BeDazzled from head to toe like disco balls. As expected, they step in our way.

"Just because you and your made-up crew made it into the competition doesn't mean you're going to win," Ivy snarls at Sally.

"And just because you look like a glitter bomb exploded

on your clothes doesn't mean you're going to shine," snaps Melissa. *Okay, Melissa is corny, but she's no pushover.*

"Yeah, why don't you guys keep it moving," adds Sally. "You smell like you need some freshening up." *Wow! Go, Sally!* The Belles slyly check their pits. They shake off their embarrassment. Maybe getting through the first two portions of the competition has given Sally a boost. Now hopefully she will think we have a shot at winning.

"Whatever, you're the one who's going to be sweating once you see our freestyle routine," says Ivy. Before they continue walking away, Brie lunges at Sally. She flinches.

"Yeah, don't freeze," says Brie. *No, she didn't.* Melissa and I start toward her, but Sally stops us.

"Let's just get ready," she insists. "They're not worth it." *Finally!* Sally's starting to really gain some confidence, and she's right. We didn't come this far to let anyone break our focus and get in the way of what we came to do: win!

When we get to our post, we stretch and go over our routine. There's no room for error. Suddenly I hear whispers from a random jumper, who points at Sally and laughs as she passes by, saying, "That's the girl who froze like an ice statue last year." I am glad that Sally doesn't hear her. She's been doing too well and staying focused. A third loud whistle sounds and the lights dim, which indicates it's time to get ready for the freestyle portion of the competition. Just as I am gathering my bag, I spot a certain someone and his crew walk into the gym. Charlie! He's supposed to be at the skateboarding competition, right? Why is he here? *Now I'm nervous.*

"No time for staring at your boyfriend, Kayla," Melissa commands. "Let's go! We gotta warm up!"

"Maybe she doesn't need a warm-up," Tina teases. "She's already got the hots."

"Ha ha, very funny," I say as I roll my eyes at her, although she's right. I have to concentrate, even if Charlie looks super-cute in his sweaty clothes, holding his skateboard. I can't believe I like a skateboard boy from the South. Suddenly Sally yanks me back into reality. Freestyle is the most important part of the competition, and if we win we'll be able to shut those bullies up, and then *maybe* they'll leave Sally alone.

All the lights are up as the next team takes the floor. It's cool they have a DJ to play music between the change of teams. It keeps fun in the air. *I'm loving it!* Each team is taking every second of their one minute to do everything and anything they can to wow the crowd. Two teams, the Hot Nonstop Steppers and the Jump Squad, have some of the crowd on their feet. *Probably family,* I think. They are pretty awesome, with a little gymnastics in their routine. A few cartwheels and back-handsprings into the ropes are cute, but they don't have nothin' on us. Wait till they see what Tina and Sally are bringing to the floor. *Huh! It's on!* I notice Sally pacing. I expected Melissa or even Tina to be this nervous, but Sally, again?

"What's going on? Are you okay?" I ask. *She's making me nervous now.*

"I'm good," Sally manages. "Just warming up."

I thought I really loved double Dutch, but it looks like my cousin loves it more than I do. It seems she's forgotten all about her reputation for being the girl who gets bullied all the time. Her friends turning their backs on her because of one mistake was a blow to her self-esteem, not to mention how sad the whole double Dutch mishap made her feel. She was embarrassed by friends she thought she could trust, but as I watch her pace, it seems like she's trying to block all that out. Today, winning means more than just a double Dutch contest. It means getting back her respect.

The Bouncing Belles are up next. Obviously they are a crowd favorite, because people are already on their feet. The judges take notice, smiling as if they're in for a treat. The Belles take the floor and wave their hands like they're all beauty queens. True Belles, I guess. I spot Aunt Jeanie and Uncle Larry in the stands. They are so supportive. I suddenly think of my parents. Why can't they be more like my aunt and uncle? Why can't my parents come to at least *one* double Dutch competition together and watch me do what I love?

As the music dies down I focus on the Belles, and I snap out of my sad thoughts. Ivy jumps first. She runs and does a double back-handspring and body-twists through the ropes, which immediately gets the crowd roaring even more. She jumps with the short Asian girl and they both do fancy footwork. Man, they are jumping and turning really fast for about thirty seconds. Now the whole crowd is on their feet watching every move intensely, except my aunt and uncle. The routine is all right so far, but it's nothing special. Until . . . wait! Melissa grabs my arm. All of our jaws drop. Ivy just did Sally's move! The jumping spider! The crowd goes wild. They finish with a quick dance step and flip into the rope simultaneously, then fall into a split while the ropes spin overhead. *Oh my G—*

"Those heffas stole your big move!" Melissa gasps. "Boo! Boo!"

"I can't believe this," Tina says, shocked.

"They spied on us!" Sally exclaims. "That day they rode past my house, they must have been watching us the whole time!"

"What? But we're up next!" I say. "This is not hap-

156

pening!" *We worked so hard.* Sally seems to be so furious that she can't even speak. Her face looks like her mind is spinning a hundred miles a minute. If I didn't know any better, I would swear there's steam coming from her head.

"Forget it!" Sally says. "So what? Maybe they did use that move, but I have another one, a better one I can do. Let's go!" *What?* I think my cousin just lost it. Sally grabs her stuff, and we follow her blazing trail to the bottom of the bleachers.

As soon as we get there, Sally turns to us with a new plan.

"Melissa, just keep your eyes on my feet," Sally says, staring into Melissa's eyes. "Kayla, I'll call it out and you can guide the ropes. Melissa will follow both of us."

"What about me?" Tina asks frantically. "What about me?"

"Be the hype girl!" I say. "No matter what we do, get the crowd into it." I have no idea what we'll be doing, but this is a do-or-die moment. I have no choice but to trust Sally on this one. I suddenly remember once when my dad, Cameron, and I were watching basketball and my dad said, *Michael Jordan was the best player of all time because under pressure he could score a basket from anywhere at any time and win the game. That's what winners do—rise when the pressure is on.* And just when I think Sally is done with her plan, she grabs a skateboard . . . from Tommy, the boy who put glue in her hair just a few days ago. I'm scared of her now. Charlie and his boys, including Tim, just stand on the sidelines watching. So I grab Charlie's skateboard and shrug. Fortunately they let us go. They have no idea what's going on and neither do I, for that matter. The crowd applauds for what seems like a year for the Belles and their stolen moves. *Ugh!*

They absorb all the cheers and head right toward us as we are on our way to take the stage.

"Real classy, stealing our big move," I say, being snarky. "That was not cool." I really feel like pushing that little *poison* Ivy into the wall, but I keep hearing Gabriella's voice in my head: *Competitors compete. . . . Fighting is for savages.* I am so hot right now!

"What?" Ivy says sarcastically. "We didn't steal anything. The jumping spider was originally a part of our routine. A part *someone* failed to pull off." She eyes Sally.

"And Ivy nailed it," adds Brie as they high-five.

"Well, apparently not, because there's a lot more where that came from. Right, Sally?" Melissa looks toward Sally, who hesitates for a second but then finds the courage to say . . .

"Yup." Sally steps up to Ivy and looks her in the eye. "The best is yet to come."

"Let's go, you guys!" yells Tina. "We're up!"

I give them a once-over and prance away. There's nothing more I can say or do but pray that we're about to blow the crowd away. And I don't even know what that is yet. *OMG!* Even though I think Sally has completely lost her mind, I am so proud of her for not giving up. Now I wonder what she can possibly have up her sleeve.

As we take the stage at the center of the gym, there's a bit of snickering and pointing. I am not sure if that's for our odd-looking squad or because they remember Sally as the girl who made their team look bad.

"You guys," commands Sally, "let's just stay focused and stay here." She points two fingers to our eyes. "Melissa and Tina, just keep your eyes on us and keep the ropes turning. We can do this! Just follow my lead." *Okay?* I sure hope she knows what she's doing. I wasn't nervous before, but I am now.

We give the DJ the thumbs-up, and we're set. The lights go dark. The best part is our costumes; they're glowing in the dark. Tina and Melissa pull the ropes from a dark bag, and they glow too. The ropes look awesome! The crowd murmurs. Sally sets down the skateboard and turns to me.

"Do exactly what I do and meet me in the ropes," a determined Sally says. Has my cousin lost her mind and I haven't noticed? But hey, I have nothing else, so I go with it.

"I'm ready," I say, not knowing what to expect, but I keep my eyes on my li'l cuz.

We both take a deep breath, and we're off.

Sally rides the skateboard across the floor and leaves the board just in time to jump into the glowing ropes. I follow right behind her. The crowd applauds. The lights come up. *And we're in!*

"Let's do it!" Melissa shouts, and takes control. "One-two-three!"

We do our footwork. Crisscross, pop up, turn front, turn back, then I grab Sally and lift her over my head as the ropes move out. We did it! The crowd jumps to their feet! *Yes!* The lights come up and I grab the ropes from Tina as she enters to do a salsa step while Melissa and I turn. Sally waves her arms, getting the crowd even more into it, then jumps in with Tina. They are killing the salsa dance as we pull the ropes to the side even without music. *Cool!* Sally then jumps out. *Wait! This is not part of the routine! What is she doing?*

"Tina! Keep following the routine!" yells Sally. "Keep turning, you guys!" Tina jumps out and pirouettes around the ropes, then jumps in. Sally sets up at the corner of the gym like she's an Olympic gymnast. I keep checking over my shoulder, as Melissa and I have no idea what's about to happen.

"Keep your eyes on her feet and let me guide the ropes!"

I yell to Melissa while Tina jumps out and cheers Sally on. Suddenly Sally flies toward us and does a somersault, a back-handspring with a twist into the ropes, then reverses the backhand into the ropes with a split while we spin the ropes behind her.

"Bring the ropes back and turn!" Sally screams. We do. Sally does four jumping splits. It's crazy! The crowd is going bananas! *Yes, Sally!* We finish our routine standing proud. The DJ adds a beat blast as if it were a cherry on top of a flawless routine.

Aunt Jeanie and Uncle Larry are going wild in the stands. They are beaming. The Bouncing Belles seem to have lost their bounce. Ivy and her crew actually look nervous. As the judges tally up the points based on all the tricks performed by all the teams, we gather our things to hear the results. *We have to win!*

A judge steps to the center of the gym with a microphone to announce . . .

"And taking third place in the regional double Dutch competition is"—the man hesitates—"the Hot Nonstop Steppers!" I breathe a sigh of relief. Our team claps, and then we cross our fingers again. I guess it's safe to say we all feel we deserve to win the whole thing.

"In second place is . . . Four-D, Double Deuces!" yells

the judge as if he's happy for us. We all jump with excitement! Although we wanted first, we realize we came a long way with two new jumpers. Sally smiles big as we head to the trophy table.

"And in first place, and still the double Dutch champions, are the Bouncing Belles!" the judge announces. The Belles run with excitement to receive their huge trophy. The crowd goes wild.

"And you're still a loser," remarks Ivy to Sally. Sally takes a huge breath and shakes her head. The feud is not over. Suddenly I think, *Ivy has issues.* Well, first place or not, we did it! Most of all, I am so proud of Sally for pulling off her own special move.

Then: "But wait, there's more!" The crowd quiets down a bit. "The two top teams are now eligible for the National Double Dutch Jump-off in New York City at Madison Square Garden!" *Did he say Madison Square Garden?* If my team in Brooklyn made it, I might have to compete against them. *No! Way!*

The Dance

To celebrate the end of camp, there's a dance, and all the competitors are invited. *A dance?* To be honest, I've never been to a dance. A house party, maybe, but not a dance. *I guess it's a small-town thing, a Southern thing.* I don't even know how to dress for a dance. So I have to ask an expert. I knock on Sally's bedroom door.

"Sally?" I ask sheepishly. She comes to the door and opens it in a huff. It looks like a tornado hit a department store and dumped all the frilly stuff in Sally's room.

"Come in, Kayla," says Sally. "I can't figure out what to wear, and my mom won't let me go to the mall to buy an outfit for this stupid dance."

"So let's not go," I say without hesitation. "I don't have anything to wear either."

"We have to go!" Sally says as she sifts through her overloaded dresser drawers. "Missing this is like missing the party of the summer. Ugh! This stuff is so old!"

"You have so many nice things," I say, picking up a boa. *What is she doing with a boa?* "I'm sure there's something you can wear. Maybe not this, but something."

"You sound like my mother," Sally says with her hands on her hips. "So what are *you* wearing? You know your boyfriend Charlie is going to be there."

"You think?" I ask genuinely. Suddenly this party is at the top of my list of things to do. *Go to dance. Check.*

"Of course," insists Sally. "Besides, there's nothing else to do in this town." As soon as I think of seeing Charlie at the dance, my stomach gets the jitters like those butterflies just got out of a cage or something.

"Well, I . . . uh . . . um," I stammer. I dare to hold one of Sally's ruffled tank tops up to myself and check the mirror.

"What's wrong with you?" Sally asks, still pulling out clothes.

I muster up the truth. "I wanna look . . . nice. Or even pretty." Sally laughs at me.

"Are you telling me you wanna look like a princess, Tomboy Cinderella?" Sally jokes. I throw the top down to the floor. This is too embarrassing! I've never worn anything frilly or sparkly or that says I'm a diva.

"Forget it. I'd look stupid anyway," I say, completely through with the idea.

"Kayla, I'm just kidding!" Sally says sincerely. "It's just I thought I'd never see the day when my tough-girl cousin wanted to look cute for some boy."

"I do not!" I protest. Sally just stares at me. "Okay, okay. So what? Are you going to help me or what?"

She looks me over once and shrugs. "Okay," she says. "One makeover coming up!"

Makeover? Is it that bad? Sally springs into action like this is something she's been waiting to do all summer, and the look of desperation on my face must have given her the hint that I really don't know where to start. As she begins picking through her pile of stuff like she is looking for gold, I think about why this "girlification," as the magazines call it, feels so weird. Growing up in a tough neighborhood in Brooklyn, I've always had to prove how strong I am. Top that with a fearless attitude, which my parents constantly tell me I was born with, and you get what people might see as a tomboy. So being a frilly girlie-girl never crossed my mind, at least not until now. When the boys back in Brooklyn catcall at me like a piece of meat, it never makes me feel special. Attention from Charlie, on the other hand, feels different, interesting even. I couldn't imagine him catcalling after girls. Charlie is more mysterious to me, and if he's really interested in me, then I want to look . . . nice, like a girl and not a tomboy.

Sally and I spend the whole afternoon trying on a thousand outfits, and nothing! We move on to the little makeup Aunt Jeanie allows us to wear. Then Sally stops and stares at my hair.

"What?" I ask.

"Those braids," Sally says. "They've got to come out." She starts for my head, but I catch her arm and pull away before she can put her hand on my braids.

"Uh-uh! Are you crazy?" I insist. "I have had my hair in braids for years. I don't know how my hair is going to look without them."

"Exactly!" Sally exclaims. "It's time for a change. Now, let me at 'em!"

Man! I let Sally help me and now she's gone crazy. I take a deep breath and cover my face as she starts taking out my braids.

"Are you going to help me?" Sally asks. "This could take all night, and we don't have that kind of time." Unwillingly I help, and Sally and I unravel my braids one by one. Although I am unconvinced, Sally helps me wash my hair and put all these products in it. After a couple of hours and a shampoo and conditioning, she fixes my hair into a style. It actually looks so . . . so pretty. Oddly I feel . . . authentic . . . like this is the real me, the way God intended me to look. It's me, but the *new* me.

"I can't believe it," I say, mesmerized by my new do. I look like I should be the model on a box of some natural hair product. "My hair looks so . . . nice. Thank you." I give my cousin a big hug.

"See, your real hair isn't bad after all." Sally smiles, then suddenly gets an idea. "Ooooh, wait!" she exclaims. "I think I know what you should wear!" She digs deep into the back of her walk-in closet. I hear a long zip, like she's unwrapping something. *Please let it be something that doesn't have glitter, rhinestones, ruffles, or feathers.* She emerges from the closet door lined with lights and holds up a beautiful blue summer dress. It's something you'd see in a fashion magazine. *Wow!* "I've been waiting to grow into this, but I think it might fit you better, since you are taller and, well, have more lady parts than me." *Is she referring to my boobies?* I don't think I've ever worn a long summer dress before, but I might be able to rock this one.

Later we arrive at the party—well, the "dance." Uncle Larry tells us to be ready to go no later than ten o'clock.

"Same spot. No later than ten," he repeats. We agree and head in to find Tina and Melissa.

The gym is beautiful now, with decorations, party favors, and silver balloons everywhere. The music is loud, and we spot Tina on the dance floor doing what she obviously loves. Melissa trots over to us in a dress that's fit for a bridesmaid.

"You guys look great! Love the hair, Kayla!" Melissa says; she looks like she wants to touch it but quickly changes her mind. "My mother made me wear my sister's old bridesmaid dress. Sucks, but, hey, thanks to double Dutch the stupid dress fits!"

"You're looking great," Sally says, "but that dress?"

I elbow Sally. "Melissa, you look beautiful!" I cover.

"Thanks! Well, I'm going to go dance. My guy is waiting." Melissa does a few pop-locks, then laughs and moonwalks away like a schoolgirl to the same boy who doused her with confetti in arts and crafts. *Go, Melissa!* I discreetly look around for Charlie but don't see him. Maybe he's too cool for camp dances. *I bet he's not going to show up.* Suddenly I feel disappointed that I got all dressed up and took my braids out for what might be nothing.

As if things couldn't get uglier, the Bouncing Belles head toward us like they have something to say. After I wave off the cloud of suffocating perfume, I cross my arms, preparing for war.

"Second place. Not bad," Ivy says.

"Yes, and it's not over," I say. "If we don't take you in New York, my girls from Brooklyn will."

"Yeah, we're scared," Brie remarks sarcastically.

"Why don't you guys give it a rest?" Sally asks. "It's getting old. Can't we at least enjoy ourselves without you trying to ruin everything?"

"Whatever. Permission granted," Ivy disses. "Let's go, girls. Party over here just took a dive."

I'm glad they leave, because I am really getting tired of their mess too. But one thing is for sure: Sally's confidence to speak up for herself is amazing now. I guess we both learned a little something from each other. She's tougher, and I'm standing here embracing my inner Beyoncé and JLo in a dress I thought I'd never wear, and I love it! And best of all, I feel pretty, even if a boy doesn't tell me to my face.

"Let's go dance!" I say to Sally as I yank her toward Tina and Melissa on the dance floor.

We dance to one song after another till we're practically sweaty. Suddenly I see Tina pointing her index finger like a blinking light. I think she's telling me to turn around, and I do. It's Charlie! *My heart skips a beat.*

"Can I have this dance?" he asks. He's so gentlemanly,

and he's dressed like a gentleman, not like the bad boys on the corner asking me if they can do things that I know I am way too young to even think about. But not Charlie.

"Sure." I bashfully giggle.

After a few songs, Charlie takes my hand and leads me outside. *Fresh air, thank goodness.* We walk around near the garden pond that I've passed by a hundred times, but tonight it feels fairy-tale romantic. Even the bugs seem to have disappeared.

"So how long will you be in Charlotte?" Charlie asks, still holding my hand.

"Until the end of the summer," I say, almost disappointed. "I guess that's another two weeks."

"Where are you from?" he asks. And then, "Don't tell me. New York?" *Okay, he's good.*

"I live in Brooklyn! How'd you know?" I ask.

"That's where my mom lives. For now, at least," Charlie answers. "Sometimes I go there in the summer, but luckily I stayed here this time." He smiles at me, and I blush at his flirtation. "You remind me of some of my stepbrother's girlfriends." Okay, I'm shocked—he goes to Brooklyn for the summer sometimes? *What?*

"Girls from New York are funny," Charlie continues.

"They act all rough and tough on the outside, but I know it's just a front."

"Really?" I ask. *Is he judging me?* "Why do you say that?"

"Because you're really just girls on the inside." Charlie smiles. *Just girls?* What the heck is that supposed to mean? "I think it's cool, though. You guys aren't easily impressed, and it makes guys step up their game. It's a challenge, and I like that." *Did he just say he likes me without saying it?* I just smile, knowing Charlie fully understands me.

"So your parents are divorced?" I ask as politely as possible.

"Yeah," he says. "Been that way for as long as I can remember. It's cool, I guess. My dad remarried, so now I have two moms. And my mom . . . well, she's another story. She was married, then divorced again, but my step-brother is still my brother, you know what I'm saying?" I nod politely. "Well, I don't mind the traveling. It's fun."

I think about my parents and how devastated I would be if they broke up. Charlie was a baby when his parents split, so he doesn't know anything different. I hang my head for a moment. I can't help but feel sad about my parents. A tear falls on my dress.

"Are you okay?" he asks. *Oh no! I'm crying!*

"It's nothing," I say. I don't want to bring him the drama.

"Want to go back inside?" Charlie asks, worried. I pull myself together and straighten up.

"I'm fine, but thanks," I say. "My parents are going through something, and I just want things to work out."

"They will." He's so confident. "You'll see." I can't believe I'm here with the boy who's been on my mind since I got here and I'm crying over what's possibly going on at home, but I can't help it. I miss my mom and dad, together, like a family, like the way things should be. I mean, how can Charlie be so sure that everything is going to be okay? I can't see how. I can't be okay with whatever happens. I don't want to grow up without a dad. And my little brother shouldn't have to either. Charlie seems like he did fine without his real mom. Maybe he sees something in being a part of two families that I don't see. *Or maybe Charlie's as magical as he seems.* I realize I've never met a boy like him before, and I am so happy I did. He makes me feel so secure. So sure. I feel his hands on my face, wiping my tears.

"I meant to tell you," Charlie says as he lifts my chin. "You . . . your hair, you look beautiful." I smile, trying to contain my heart, which beats faster and faster. I look down again, and again he lifts my chin like he is going to . . . Oh my gosh! Is he leaning toward me . . . ? Is he going to kiss me? Time stops. Oh my . . . *Wow! Oh wow!* What feels like an eternity of complete shock, like

172

joy on Christmas morning, like trying to calm the wild butterflies in my stomach, is the moment I have my first kiss. *Boom! Boom! Boom!* We both jump back. Are those fireworks? I can't tell if it is my mind flipping out over the kiss or if I really am seeing fireworks. It's both! Besides my heart throbbing out of control, the camp is putting on a fireworks show.

Charlie and I look back at each other and lean in to continue the kiss—until we hear laughter. A moment later, Sally, Tina, and Melissa fall from behind a tree. Melissa and Tina laugh hysterically, while Sally isn't too happy as she dusts off her dress. Charlie just shakes his head. I think my face is still frozen. I am still floating on cloud nine . . . another concept I never understood until now. *It's really nice up here.* He grabs my hand and pulls me all the way back into the gym and we dance, and dance, and dance!

Mix and Match

I wake up the next morning in a haze. I try to get up but fall back and stare out the window at the pretty blue Carolina sky, daydreaming about Charlie. I'm not sure, but I think Cameron might have come into the room to talk to me. If he did, I don't remember a word he said. He could've grown six inches taller and sprouted a mustache for all I know. I wonder if I ate. I don't think we had anything to eat at the dance. We were busy having too much fun. Then it hits me.

I'll be going home soon, and I wonder if we'll be in the double Dutch competition in New York. We're eligible, but does that mean there's another competition we have to win? *I don't know.* But then I think of the kiss again, and that we all danced until the dance was over. Charlie is much sillier than the serious boy I first met. He gave me his phone number even though my parents won't let me have a phone yet. *That's just not cool.* As I stare at the old house phone on the wall, I want to call him right now. Then I remember my mom saying that when a boy really likes a girl, she doesn't have to be so eager. That he'll find a way to her. *Ugh!* But being patient is so hard, and I'm going to miss Charlie so much! I wonder if I'll see him again before I leave Charlotte. *I sure hope so.*

I can vaguely hear my uncle and aunt outside talking loudly about patio furniture. The pool is almost done, and now they're decorating and fussing over colors, pillows, umbrellas, and other stuff. Their arguing sounds nothing like my mom and dad's arguments, so there's nothing to cry about. The chattering begins to take a backseat to more daydreaming of Charlie until . . . Sally busts open the bedroom door.

"We gotta go!" urges Sally. "Get up, Kayla! Let's go!"

"What?" I'm so groggy. "Where are we going?" I'm trying to shake off this country sleep coma. I don't even know if I'm awake or dreaming.

"Come on! Get up! The competition people are at the camp!" Sally yells from her room.

"What competition people?" I still haven't shaken off

the sleep. She pops into the doorway with her hands on her hips.

"The double Dutch competition!" Sally says. "Did you lose your mind last night?" Maybe. "Well, you better get Charlie off your brain 'cause we have business down at the camp *now!*" What's gotten into her? Did I create a monster?

"Charlie who?" Aunt Jeanie says from down the hall. *Well, this is embarrassing.* She comes into view behind Sally.

"No one!" I shout as I jump out of bed.

"Charlie Davis?" Aunt Jeanie asks again. "That's cute. He used to be Sally's little crush." I quickly look at Sally. *I knew it!* Why didn't she tell me?

"Ma!" Sally leaves in a huff, embarrassed. Aunt Jeanie thinks it's funny. And mothers wonder why we don't like telling them anything.

"Charlie and Sally went to the same elementary school, and she used to talk about him all the time. How cute he was and how all the girls tripped over themselves for him." She goes on. "And I guess he's got you under his spell too, huh? This is too cute." Aunt Jeanie has no idea the can of worms she just opened up, even if she thinks it's so "cute." Sally's not acting like her crush is fully over. "Well, come on, lady, have some lunch before you two head out."

On our way to the gym, Sally rides her bike a lot faster than usual. I can barely keep up with her.

"Wait up!" I scream. "Sally, I didn't know!" She doesn't answer me. I speed up and get ahead of her. She slows down as I pull my bike in front of hers. She stops.

"I'm sorry! I didn't know you liked him," I say. "Why didn't you just say something?"

"I didn't say anything because there's nothing to say. It's no big deal!" insists Sally. "Charlie likes you and not me and that's it." I don't think that's it. She's hiding something.

"I just don't want you to be mad at me," I say sincerely. "We've actually become friends this summer. I mean, you're my cousin, but you know what I mean. It's cool being friends." Sally just looks around. "So are we cool?" She hesitates, then:

"It's that I really used to like him since second grade, like almost every girl in this town, and he never paid me any mind," she admits. "Then you come around and he kisses *you*—right in front of me! I thought I'd be okay with it, but when I saw it happen, I guess I wasn't." I don't know what to say. I just stare at her. "I guess I'm just . . . jealous." *Wait a minute . . . My cousin. Is. Jealous. Of. Me?* I take a moment to think before I speak, something I've never done before, but she's my cousin and I think it's best to go easy on her feelings. I need to say the right thing or else things could get ugly between us again, and honestly I really don't want that.

"Well, he *is* a cute boy. I think anybody would be jealous of any girl he likes," I say.

"Yeah, that's true, but you're my cousin and it's just a little . . ."

"Awkward?" I finish her sentence.

"Yeah, awkward," agrees Sally.

"If you had told me in the beginning, maybe I wouldn't have paid him any attention," I say. "But you made it seem like you were okay with him liking me. You were the one who even pointed it out. You know what, forget it. I'll just tell him to leave me alone." I cringe inside because I *really* like Charlie, but Sally's my cousin, and like Aunt Jeanie said when I first got here, we're family, whether we like it or not.

"No, don't do that!" Sally says. "I mean, admitting I was jealous would've sounded stupid. So I just thought I shouldn't say anything."

"Sally, being jealous isn't stupid," I say. "I mean, I've always been jealous of you." Sally listens up. "The way I see it . . . you have everything. Your mom and dad get along, and they pay attention to you. You have an older brother who's got your back, and you practically have everything you want. Why do you think I make fun of you and call

178

you a princess all the time?" I look away. "I've never been treated like a princess."

"I'm sorry." She tries to console me.

"Sally, that's nothing to apologize for. That's just the way it is, and it's okay. I'm the one who has to deal with it."

"Just like I have to deal with the fact that Charlie likes you and not me," she sighs.

"I guess that's just how life works, huh?" I conclude.

"Well, at least we're better than we were when we were little." Sally smirks a bit, and I smile back.

"Yeah, but you played with baby dolls!" I laugh.

"I was seven!" Sally laughs. "And you took all my baby dolls and threw them into the tree."

"I wanted us to climb the tree, build a tree house or something," I say with a smile. "I thought if I put your babies in the tree, we'd have fun climbing up there to get them, but no. You sat and cried and I got in trouble."

"I had fifteen dolls!" Sally yells.

"And I was bored!" I yell back as I hop onto my bike. Sally follows. "But you have to admit, Baby Alive pooping on your face was pretty funny."

"To you it was." Sally smirks. "I had just fed her chocolate pudding too."

As we ride to the gym, we reminisce about some of the craziest things we did when we were little. I'm just glad my cousin isn't mad at me over a boy—the neighborhood

It boy, but a boy nonetheless. We hustle to the gym to make up for lost time.

At the camp, it's weird not to see everyone running around. It's like a ghost town, but there are cars parked outside the gym, so we head inside with the bikes.

The divas are there, sprawled on the floor, stretching. Melissa and Tina run to our side.

"They're talking about putting us together!" Tina starts right in.

"What?" Sally asks.

"Why? We already have our team," I add.

"Hi, girls," a voice from across the room calls. "Why don't you come in and sit down."

There are two people, a guy and a girl, both dressed in jeans and button-down shirts, semibusiness, I guess. I've never seen them before, but they look somewhat official. Our team settles down on the gym floor across from the Belles. And like a jar of nutty peanut butter, the air is still thick and rough. Now I'm starting to sound country like my uncle Larry. We pretend to be on our best behavior, and we pay attention to Coach Kirsten.

"Okay, you guys," she says. "You know I'm Coach Kirsten, but I've been coaching the Belles outside of camp for . . ."

"Well, that's not fair!" Melissa starts right away.

"Well, where's your coach? Oh, you don't have one, and who are you, again?" Ivy retorts.

Melissa is up on her feet. Tina, Sally, and I jump to join her. The Belles are on their feet too. We're all yelling at each other, mostly saying how we can't stand each other. Kirsten steps in the middle.

"Quiet down, you guys!" she demands. "Everyone sit down!" We all do, out of respect. "Now, I can help you guys get into this competition or not. What's it going to be?" We all murmur in agreement. "All right, that's more like it," she continues. "I know you guys love double Dutch or you wouldn't be here."

"Got that right" slips out of my mouth.

"Please don't sass." Kirsten gives me a sharp look. With attitude, I zip my lips.

The couple standing in the back comes forward as some sort of representatives of the National Double Dutch League. They explain the rules to us and that there's a new part of the competition called fusion. It's kind of like freestyle, but you can have a maximum of six jumpers and there can be dance, acrobatics, and music incorporated, crammed into a two-minute routine. Sounds like crazy fun!

"Wait!" I suddenly have a question. "There's four of them and four of us?"

"You guys are going to have to drop someone," Brie says matter-of-factly.

"I suggest Sally," Ivy says. The Belles laugh.

"I wouldn't be on the same team with you if you paid me," says Sally with dignity.

"No one wants to be on their team," chimes in Tina. "They're so mean."

"We're not mean! We just don't want to work with amateurs!" Ivy says.

"Call us amateurs one more time . . . ," Melissa threatens, and the arguing in the gym gets loud again. I just want to fill Ivy's face with my fist but restrain myself. That little girl is not worth me embarrassing myself or, worse, getting in trouble for beating up some Southern girl with all that mouth. I feel the old me suddenly creeping back into my veins, but I'm not going to let her do it. *I'm not gonna do it!* Kirsten whistles really loudly. We calm down and sit back on the gym floor.

"There's not enough time for this childishness. If you guys want to compete, you're going to have to work together," insists Kirsten. "Now, Sally, I know there's some history with this team, but it's time we all bury the hatchet and move on." Sally and Ivy share a look and try not to show any emotion, but I can tell they were once the best of friends. "I've been informed that two of the Belles won't be able to make the trip because of family vacation conflicts." Two of the Belles slowly put up their hands to indicate whom Kirsten is referring to. Ivy and Brie shoot them a look and moan in disgust. "Now, if you guys don't join forces, you won't be able to compete in fusion, and the sponsors won't pay for the trip."

"What sponsors?" I ask.

"*Our* sponsors," says Brie.

"Well, excuse me," I say, surprised, as I hold my hands up. The Belles just smirk like they're special because they have "sponsors." Well, it is kind of special, considering they only just finished seventh grade, but I'm not showing them I'm impressed. Not after the way they've treated my cousin.

"So, do we have a deal?" asks Kirsten.

I turn to the rest of my team and create a huddle. It is clear that the last thing we want to do is work with the enemy, but competing on a higher level and a trip to Madison Square Garden, which of course is what I've been wanting all summer, seem like no-brainers. Then I have a thought: *Who's going to coach us?* So we come to a conclusion: we are in under one condition.

"We get a coach too," I say with my arms crossed. My girls back me up with their arms crossed too.

"That's right. If we have someone who knows how to work with us, we're in," says Sally. "No offense."

Their coach looks more confused than insulted.

"Sure," Kirsten says with her eyebrows raised. "Who do you have in mind?"

"Her name is Gabriella, and she's good," Melissa says

with a smile, like she knows what she's talking about. Kirsten tilts her head to the side like she recognizes the name.

"They can't bring their own coach, can they?" asks Brie. "That's just rude."

"Gabriella who?" Kirsten asks suspiciously.

"Gabriella Upton," Sally answers. Kirsten's eyes roll back in her head. *Hmm . . . I take it she knows Gabriella.*

"Okay." Kirsten throws her hands up. "Okay, if that's what you want. I guess we'll all just have to work together." I could be assuming, but it seems like Ms. Kirsten and Ms. Gabriella are going to have to bury a hatchet themselves. *This is going to be interesting.*

I don't think these girls understand they're going to New York, where the competition is going to be thick. If we're going to even have a chance, especially against my friends back home—which is going to be crazy awkward—we're really going to have to focus. Hopefully we'll be able to get Gabriella on board. I wonder if she'll do it knowing Kirsten is in charge of the Bouncing Belles.

I'm going to the Garden!

Pool Party

It's Sunday, and instead of taking us to brunch after church, Uncle Larry says we're heading home for an announcement. I just love how my uncle and aunt make everything a "surprise" or an "announcement." So far I've liked every surprise, so I'm looking forward to this one. Even going to church was a surprise, but then again I've heard that a family that prays together stays together, which I always wished for my family. But while I've been here, I have prayed so hard that things would go okay: with my parents, that we'll win the competition at Madison Square Garden; I even prayed for Sally. I hope she heard everything the preacher was saying about refusing to be fearful, to always be strong and have courage because God is always with you. I have never told anyone, but it's my secret weapon. I use it against anything and anyone who tries to hurt me—ever since third grade, when I read the Bible for the first time with my mom. Since then I've never let anyone bully me or anything scare me, even the stuff with my mom and dad. If they break up, I will be sad, but eventually I know I'll be okay. It's just not what I want for me and Cameron. But that's just me. I never told Sally about my weapon, because I didn't want her to think I was some Jesus freak, but maybe I am . . . on the inside. I guess I just try to practice it before I go preaching it, since I never want to act like I am holier-than-thou. Hopefully she'll learn sooner than later who's *really* got her back.

When we arrive at the house, Uncle Larry announces that after three hot weeks of summer, the pool is finally finished! And while we were at the camp yesterday, Aunt Jeanie sneakily planned a surprise pool party! Melissa and Tina are at the house with their pool toys and ready to go in no time. And to my and Sally's surprise, Auntie invited Charlie and some of his friends!

I can't believe it. There he is . . . in his swimming trunks . . . with a big Super Soaker water gun. *Um . . .*

yeah! Butterflies. I didn't have time to think about how cute I look in this one-piece bathing suit Aunt Jeanie picked up for me.

But I suddenly feel weird about the mosquito bites on my legs. I completely forgot about the tiny vampires of the South that multiply like New York City fruit flies. They're everywhere, just waiting to drain my double Dutch legs of their beauty. Now I look like I have the chicken pox. *Yuck!* I try to cover up without looking awkward. I guess I look okay, because Charlie is watching my every move.

Sally and I just wave as we set down our towels on the new patio lounge chairs. I feel like I'm back at the beach resort my dad took us to once, when we went to Disney World when I was six. Luckily three of Charlie's friends have come too, including the one who seemed to like Sally, so hopefully there won't be any awkwardness between us over Charlie. I try to play it cool and not act so nervous as I walk to the edge of the pool, but I almost trip over my own two feet like I even forgot how to walk. Now I know what Auntie meant by "girls tripping over themselves."

But before we can dip our toes in the water, Uncle Larry makes the eight of us, plus my anxious little brother and Sally's two brothers, wait until he finds his whistle. It's starting to feel more like a celebration for him, since his summer project is finally complete. But with every passing second of us standing in the sun, the temperature outside can't get any hotter. With the boys on one side, we all start fidgeting around and sneaking peeks at each other like second graders playing peekaboo. Suddenly Uncle Larry pops out of the sliding doors with his whistle in the side of his mouth.

"Are you sharks ready to swim?" he asks. "Hold on. You all know how to swim, right?" Everyone nods and yells yes except me. I can flop around like a fish out of water pretty good, but I definitely can't swim. So I raise my hand to confess.

"Well, I'm not quite sure—" I say.

"I'll teach her." Charlie cuts me off. All my teammates giggle as Uncle Larry looks at him. Sally smiles and nods as if to say, *It's cool.*

"Kayla, stay on the shallow side," Uncle Larry says. "I'll be watching you, boy." He points at Charlie, who just grins kindly. *Uncle Larry is so funny!* "Ready, on three! Everybody count with me."

"One-two-three!" We all jump in! *Yeeeeesss!!*

Not long after we jump in, Marc and Gabriella show up with beach balls and all kinds of water gadgets. Sally and the team look at each other, knowing that before the day is over we'll have to ask Gabriella to coach us. I think we all want to jump out of the pool and ask her right away, but we are having so much fun and we are right in the middle of water tag. *Too fun!* Besides, I haven't had any time alone with Charlie. Just tagging "You're it!" is all we can think about right now.

While we play hours of water guns, Marco Polo, and water volleyball, and just float around on lounge floaties, Uncle works himself into a frenzy over the grill. Thank goodness, because I am hungry!

"Come on, you crumb snatchers!" Uncle Larry shouts. "Come get some grub!"

We can't get out of the pool fast enough, but as soon as I try to climb out, I'm unexpectedly pulled back in. *Ugh! Charlie!* He laughs and I splash water in his face. He splashes back. A splash fight! Everyone is egging us on. Until I hear: *"Kayla!"* It's Aunt Jeanie calling me. We stop, but not before water splashes her too. Charlie and I gasp.

"Sorry, Aunt Jeanie," I say through a tight smile. She just blinks hard to avoid getting water in her eyes, and then wipes her hair back.

"Your mother is on the phone, sweetie," Aunt Jeanie says, regaining her dignity.

My mother? All of a sudden my smile turns into a wide-eyed stare. I am no longer hungry, and a bunch of questions rush through my mind: Why is she calling? What's wrong? Are my parents going to tell me and Cameron they're getting a divorce?

"Cameron!" I shout. "Let's go!" I don't know why, but I think he should be with me. Who knows what kind of news I am going to get, but I don't want to be alone. This is a family thing, and even though he's only seven he should know the verdict.

I rush to the kitchen and grab the phone from the counter. Those butterflies in my stomach are balled up in a knot.

"Hello?" I say. "Hi, Mom, how are you? I miss you. Are you doing okay?" I can't help the things flying out of my mouth.

"Hi, baby!" Mom says. "Wow! Don't you sound all grown up." She sounds happy. Well, happier than when I left Brooklyn.

"She better not be that grown up," says a male voice.

"Daddy?" I cry.

"Hey, baby girl, I had to call and check on you. Make sure you're keeping your cool down there," says my dad sweetly. "And how's Cameron? Is he behaving himself?"

"Yes, I think he's grown an inch," I answer, but I don't want to talk about Cameron, who grabs at the phone; I dodge him while I'm trying to find the words to get some answers.

"So I hear you and Sally are getting along better," says Mom. "That's really good to hear, sweetie."

"Yeah, I'm actually having fun," I admit. "It's not like I remember at all."

"What about this little boy I'm hearing about?" asks Dad. "Do I have to come down there with my shotgun?" My dad's jokes can be funny and scary at the same time. It depends on whether he's smiling . . . or maybe not. It's hard to tell with him. But my aunt must've said something, since she thinks everything is cute with me and Sally.

"Um." I giggle.

"Um, what?" my dad says.

"Nothing, Dad." I smile. "Remember you said that when I get to junior high I can have a phone? So can I have a phone now?"

"I'm assuming so you can call this boy, huh?" he asks. "Yeah, I'm gonna have to pull out the shotgun."

"Johnnie, leave her alone," my mom says. "We'll see about that when you get home, baby. And, Johnnie, I know my girl has been a perfect lady, but she and I will talk more privately when she's home." *Uh-oh! Not the talk.* I already know where babies come from, and I didn't learn it at home. A girl at my school was supposedly pregnant, which is crazy because she is around my age. The rumors that swirled were unbelievable and sad, but I think my whole grade learned that boys and girls can make babies

191

even if they are just becoming teenagers. I felt sorry for the girl, but I never found out what really happened. She was so brave about everything, but I just remembered saying to myself, *I wouldn't want that to happen to me.* So that was another reason why I didn't think about boys— well, until I met Charlie.

"Well, this boy better keep his hands to himself, if he knows what's good for him," my dad continues. *Okay, Dad!*

"I can handle myself, Dad."

"Well, okay," says Mom.

"So are you, um . . ." Before I can find the words to ask about them and what they've decided, Cameron starts to tug at the phone. "Cameron, stop."

"I want to talk too," insists Cameron. But I haven't told them how I made it to the double Dutch finals. Did my aunt tell them? Why didn't they mention it? Do they even care?

"Let me speak to my boy," Dad says before I can ask my question and get an answer. I just sigh and let Cameron have the phone.

"Hi, Mommy! Are you coming here?" Cameron asks excitedly. "Daddy!" I've never seen my little brother so excited to speak to my dad before. He may be young, but I think he understands what's going on.

Ding-dong-ding-dong-ding-dong! I walk to the front door

because someone is ringing the bell as if they like pushing buttons. And I am right. . . . Because when I open the door, I see four Bouncing Belles in their sunglasses and bathing suits. *Uh, what?* I hear Aunt Jeanie calling Sally to the door. Sally comes running, not knowing what to expect, but opens the door wider to see her enemies. I think every drop of pool water evaporates off her face at that very moment. I stand there with her. *I've got her back.*

"Can I help you?" asks Sally, trying to be polite.

"We heard there was pool party and we were invited," Ivy says smugly. "And a party's not a party unless we're there."

"Invited? By who?" Sally asks. Brie looks toward Aunt Jeanie, who pretends not to be watching or listening. She's whistling about her business as she stirs the iced tea. She stops and looks up at us.

"Well, I thought it would be a good idea, since you are going to be on the same double Dutch team and all," Aunt Jeanie says matter-of-factly.

Sally looks at Ivy, then at me, as if she's thinking of the best way to handle this. Then: *Slam!* She slams the door right in their faces. *I didn't see that coming!* We high-five like we one-upped them big-time. Aunt Jeanie doesn't say a word but shoots Sally a fiery look and stands with one hand on her hip. *Now I see where Sally gets that stance from.*

"I know, Mama, but it's time they stop bullying," Sally says.

"I couldn't agree more. And now is the perfect opportunity for you to set the record straight," Aunt Jeanie says as she gathers the tea on a tray. "I trust you'll do the right thing." She grabs the tea and heads out back to the pool. She was a little wrong for inviting Sally's bullies over without telling her first, but what she said was right. It's time for Sally to settle this once and for all.

"So what are you going to do?" I ask. Sally stares blankly at me, then quickly swings open the door. Ivy, Brie, and their team are still standing there.

"I knew you'd come to your senses," Ivy says. "Come on, guys! I smell Mr. Walker's barbecue." Sally steps in her way before Ivy and the other Belles can set foot in the house.

"Not so fast," Sally says. "Is there anything else you and your friends would like to say to me before I let you back into my house?"

Ivy sulks, and then she leans over Sally's shoulder to whisper in her ear.

"Look, I'm sorry, okay?" Ivy says discreetly.

"No, not okay!" Sally says loudly. "You guys kicked me off the team because I made one mistake. And then you've picked on me every day since. Do you know what that's done to me? I've become free game for anyone who wants to pick on me at school."

"We kicked you off the team because you messed up our chance to go to New York *last* summer," says Ivy.

"So you wouldn't be here if you didn't have to work with me and my new team?"

"Maybe not," Ivy says, still acting smug. Sally steps closer to Ivy, who backs up from the entrance. Suddenly Sally seems different: tougher, stronger, and definitely braver. It's like she's even standing taller.

"Well, if you were really my friend from the beginning, you would've had my back. You would've helped me, you would've told me, 'It's okay, there's always next year,' something, anything. But instead you chose to treat me like I had no feelings, like we hadn't known each other since second grade. *I* was the first kid to make friends with you. You were my best friend in the whole world, and I thought you were a good person, but you're not. You're a fraud, because good friends don't bully friends!" Sally turns to walk away with tears falling from her eyes. I guess all those hurt feelings finally came out right there at the front door.

"Wait!" calls Ivy, holding back tears. Sally slowly turns around. Ivy looks for permission to enter the house. Sally tilts her head to the side, I guess to show it's okay. Ivy looks at me as she passes, and I stare right at her as if to say, *That's right, I still have my eyes on you, girl.* She then looks back to Sally.

"I'm sorry. I'm truly sorry," insists Ivy. "I was so mad at you because I know how good you are and we really wanted to go to New York to compete. But once we started making fun of you and everyone else started making fun, I couldn't stop. I guess I didn't want anyone to think I was weak."

"So you're a follower and you pretended to be mean?" asks Sally. "Don't you know being mean to someone doesn't make you look strong or cool? It makes you look weak and stupid."

"Okay, maybe I was mad or jealous because the coach gave you the solo and not me!" Ivy confesses. "I thought I deserved it, but she gave it to you, and then you froze like a block of ice."

"I don't know what happened. I freaked out because I thought I couldn't do it," Sally admits. "The pressure of everyone expecting me to be so good got to me." There's a silence as they both think about that moment, I suppose. Then Sally lightens up. "But it was pretty funny."

"When you think about it, it really was funny," says Ivy. "You stood there like an ice sculpture. Seriously." Ivy pretends to be frozen. Sally gives her a blank stare, but seconds later they both bust out laughing.

"And what's worse is that I couldn't hear a thing. All those eyes on me, I almost fainted! It was so crazy." They keep laughing.

"So are we cool again?" Ivy asks sheepishly.

"It depends. Are you, Brie, and your whole team going to stop bullying me?" Sally asks boldly and loudly. Ivy looks at her friends and they all shamefully nod. "So you promise I won't have any problem in or out of school?" Again, they all nod. "Good. Now we're good." Sally smiles and holds out her hand to shake on it, but to her surprise Ivy gives her a hug. Maybe all that fronting she was doing for her friends was exhausting. Suddenly Melissa and Tina burst into the kitchen.

"She said yes!" Tina exclaims.

"Gabriella's going to coach us!" shouts Melissa, then notices the Belles. "What are they doing here?"

"They're here for the party." Sally smiles at Ivy. Well, I guess now we're one big team. The Belles rush through the door, straight out to the pool. I hope Ivy and her friends were telling the truth, but we'll see how things go when we finally get to work to prepare for the competition. *We're going to New York together!* Then I remember I left my brother on the phone with my parents. *Oh no!* I run to Cameron, who's just hanging up.

"They said they'll call back later," says Cameron as he hands me a dead phone. But I didn't get to ask them if they're going to get a divorce. I guess I'll just have to forget about it and wait until the time comes. Like Charlie said, everything will work out. *I can only hope.*

After we eat, the pool calls to us to jump back in, so we do. Without all the tension between us and the Belles, we're able to get along like nothing ever happened. Music plays as Aunt Jeanie enjoys a glass of wine, the way my mom does after a hard day's work, smiling out of the side of her mouth. I think she is happy to see Sally and her old friends getting along again. She's probably especially happy for Sally. Aunt Jeanie knows what a relief it must be to have her best friend back. As for me, I'm glad I didn't get in a fight with anyone. Now that I think about it, fighting would've just been plain stupid. My mother will be happy to know that I've learned to keep my cool and not get in trouble, let things work themselves out. I hope they call back tonight. I have so much to talk to my mom about. And I want to know: are we still a family or not?

By the time the sun goes down, some of the Belles and others leave, but nothing takes my attention away from Charlie. He is teaching me how not to flop around like a fish out of water, to really swim. We are in the pool for so long our fingers are beginning to look like shriveled raisins. Then: *Flash!* We jump as if we saw a shark, but it is just the pool lights.

"Like that?" Uncle Larry boasts. "You guys weren't ready for it, but *bam!* There it is!" Uncle Larry laughs like maybe he's had too much wine. These lights are so bright you probably can see them from outer space. Charlie and I get out of the pool and sit in the only seat available. I call it a snuggle seat, because it's round and if two people get in, the only thing you can do is snuggle. I glance over to see if my aunt or uncle might have something to say about me being snuggly with a boy, but they seem too busy playing some kind of card game with Gabriella and Marc. And my little cousins are teaching Cameron how to catch fireflies. They're so pretty when they light up at night, but if one crawled near me, I'd freak out.

"So you'll be leaving pretty soon?" Charlie asks.

"Yeah, I can't say I'm happy about going home," I say. "I can't believe I just said that."

"Maybe you'll come back next summer," says Charlie. "Or maybe I'll see you in Brooklyn." Did *he* just say that?

"Seriously?" I ask. "When?"

"I don't know," responds Charlie. "My mom hasn't figured out which holiday she wants me to spend with her. I don't think she even knows what she'll be doing next.

It's hard to explain, so I don't say much about my mother. I just visit without expecting anything to be the same or different."

"I thought you liked your mom," I say.

"I love my mother," Charlie says. "Let's just say I go with the flow when it comes to my mom." If I wasn't mystified by him before, I am now. The way he looks at life is so intriguing. Maybe that's what happens with divorced kids; they grow up a little faster than others and learn more because they have two separate families teaching them different things. "But I go and eat all the pizza I can. Brooklyn has the best pizza," he adds.

"That's very true. Well, there's good pizza in Manhattan too." I laugh. "And Queens . . . you'll just have to come to New York! I'll take you to this place in Queens that has the best, *best* pizza you'll ever have! My dad took us there once."

"I think I know a place in Queens too," Charlie says. "I was kind of small, so I'm not sure if I remember. Anyway, going to New York will be more exciting now that I know you'll be there." I can't help but blush.

"Thanks," I say as I look away, unable to meet his eyes.

"Well, I have to get going. My stepmom doesn't like me riding my skateboard late at night." My heart sinks. This will probably be the last time I see him unless he comes to Brooklyn next summer. *Wishful thinking.*

We must have been sitting there for a long time, because all of Charlie's friends have left. My little brother and cousins are back in the pool, and Sally and Ivy are hanging out on the swings, probably catching up. As Charlie gathers his things and says good night to my aunt and uncle, I head inside to the "powder room," as my aunt calls it. I check the mirror to make sure the last time Charlie looks at my face I won't have something crawling out of my nose or that my skin doesn't look ashy. Just to be safe, I pump some sweet-smelling lotion from the hand soap set that sits on the counter and rub it all over my face, then check my breath to make sure I don't smell like the onions on my burger. I read in some magazine that the biggest turnoff to boys is stinky breath.

Uncle Larry is walking Charlie to the door. *Oh, Uncle Larry!* I hope he's not going to make sure he leaves without letting me say good-bye.

"Good seeing you, son," says Uncle Larry. "And tell your father I said to stop by sometime—take a dip in the pool."

"I will, Mr. Walker," says Charlie, who sees me standing behind my uncle. Uncle Larry turns around to find me.

"Oh, uh, I'll leave you two." Uncle Larry tiptoes away. "But I'm not too far. I'm watching y'all." I smile at him. I love that he trusts me enough to give me at least a little privacy.

As soon as I close the door behind me, Charlie plants a kiss right on my lips. I wasn't ready, but I see fireworks again, even though there aren't any real ones this time.

"Whoa," I say as he backs up and stares into my eyes. "That was . . ."

"I like you," says Charlie. "And I don't like saying good-bye." I try to catch my breath before I can say anything.

"So . . . say you'll see me after practice tomorrow," I say cleverly.

"I can't," Charlie says, disappointed. "My team is going to Raleigh to compete at this crazy skateboard park. It's going to be awesome." *Skateboarder, right.*

"Well, say you'll see me in New York and that we'll have pizza in Brooklyn, or Manhattan, or in Queens," I plead.

"Now, that would be cool, but I don't like making promises," says Charlie. I hang my head. *Does he want to see me again or not?* "But if I'm in New York anytime soon, I will definitely call you." *Well, maybe he does.*

"Okay," I sigh. I really want him to come to New York. I want him to be there when I get back. "I'm gonna miss you." There, I admitted it out loud.

"No, you're not, because you're going to call me as soon as you get home," he says as he puts one foot on his board. I can't help it. I practically leap into his arms and kiss him again and again and again. I want to absorb his smell, his

202

energy, anything I can remember him by. *Porch light!* I see a shadow, but I can't make out who it is; I think someone's trying to tell me my boyfriend time is up.

"I better get inside," I say as I hug him one more time, then back away.

Charlie takes one long look at me, then takes off. *Right, no good-byes.* I watch him until he disappears under the streetlights. Letting out a big sigh helps me get my breathing back to normal again, but my heart? Well, that's going to take some time.

Bright Ropes, Big City

With the Belles and 4-D meeting for the first time as friends at practice, it feels weird, but cool, I guess. However, for our two coaches, Kirsten and Gabriella, it isn't smooth sailing right away. I was right when I had a feeling these two had a hatchet to bury.

"Well, well, well," says Gabriella as she sets eyes on Kirsten.

"Well, well, well, yourself, Gabriella Upton," Kirsten says with crossed arms.

"Kirsten Dunlap, how have you been?" Gabriella asks as she stretches out her hand. Kirsten looks at us, the new double Dutch team before her, and hesitates. Then she shakes Gabriella's hand.

"I've been well since we last met and my team took home the state championship trophy for best cheer squad," Kirsten says through gritted teeth.

"Of course you did, after stealing our routine," Gabriella says, also through gritted teeth. "Of course you did."

The rest of us girls look at each other like, *What?* Feeling the thick and familiar tension, I see Sally and Ivy whispering to each other. While Kirsten and Gabriella obviously have flashbacks of their high school rivalry, Sally and Ivy stand up.

"Hey! We have an idea," Ivy says.

"Yeah, since we're a new team, why don't we come up with a new name and start over," suggests Sally.

"This way we all can have a fresh start," says Ivy. "You know, like put all the bad stuff behind us and work together?" It's like Sally and Ivy are attempting to act like adults, telling Kirsten and Gabriella to do the right thing. Not to mention it is weird seeing them be real friends and on the same team again.

"Yeah, there're going to be a lot of great teams there, and we won't have a chance unless we really work hard together," Sally adds.

For whatever it's worth, Kirsten and Gabriella roll their

eyes and look at one another. Kirsten extends her hand first this time.

"Truce?" asks Kirsten.

"Looks like we've got our work cut out," answers Gabriella. Kirsten smiles as they shake hands.

"You heard her, ladies," Kirsten announces. "On your feet!"

Yes! Finally we get to combine our ideas and collaborate on the best routine we can possibly put together! We have lots of decisions to make . . . who's turning, who's jumping, who can do anything extra, like acrobatics, what music we are going to use, what's our dance, can *they* dance, do we do a chant or not, when does the music start and stop and start again, what are our costumes going to look like, and then, most important . . . who's going to do a solo? That's when time seems to slow down.

"Well, let's think about this one," suggests Kirsten.

"Count me out," says Sally. "I don't want that kind of pressure again. No thank you."

"Now, wait a minute, Sally," says Gabriella. "Are you sure? I mean, just because you messed up before doesn't mean you shouldn't try again."

"I don't know," Brie chimes in. "I'm all for second chances, but we're going to be in New York. It's not an easy crowd."

"You've got a point there," agrees Kirsten.

"Thanks, Gabriella," says Sally. "I thought I could do it last time, but I don't want to mess up again and let everyone down. I vote for Ivy to have the solo."

"Okay," says Gabriella. "But there's nothing like proving to yourself that you can do it." *If I was Sally, I would fight to redeem myself, but as my mother told me, you can't force people to act the way you want them to act. I know Sally can do it, but I'm not going to pressure her.*

"What about Kayla?" suggests Melissa. "It's her hometown, and she's good too. I mean really good." *Aw!*

"Thanks, Melissa!" I smile wide. "But I think I'll stick to speed. Maybe Ivy should have the solo this time, like Sally said." *I just don't want to get on my cousin's bad side again. It's bad enough Charlie likes me, not Sally. I don't want to chance showing her up at double Dutch too. Not a good idea. Besides, Sally is the one who has to see these girls every day at school, so I can see why she would want to keep the peace and hand it over to Ivy. Double Dutch politics, I guess.*

"Okay, Ivy, you're it!" Kirsten confirms. Ivy jumps and cheers for herself. *I've seen her jump and she's got talent, but this national competition is going to be on a whole other level, especially since it's really an international competition. She can talk the talk, but can she walk the walk . . . in New York?*

Finally Cameron and I are going home! *I am so ready for this!* But I'm not sure I'm ready for the verdict from my parents. Are they still together, or are they really going to split up? What will happen to me and Cameron? Why didn't they call back? They didn't even congratulate me for getting into the double Dutch finals. As I get back to Aunt Jeanie and Uncle Larry's house, I run upstairs to my room and grab the phone. I can't take it anymore! All this time I have been telling Sally how she needs to stand up to her bullies and not let things get in the way of her happiness. But what about me? What about my happiness? What about what I want? I want my family to stay together!

The phone rings and, typically, no one answers. I try my mom's cell. She doesn't answer. I call my dad's cell. He doesn't answer. Where are they? Why aren't they answering? What if it was an emergency? My heart is beating so hard and tears are welling up in my eyes. I dial the house again. *Beep!*

"Mom and Dad, it's me, MaKayla," I say. "Cameron and I have been down here for almost a month and you haven't told us anything. You sent us down here because you've been fighting, but you haven't even told us what's going to happen. You guys act like we don't matter! Cam

208

and I matter! I made it to the double Dutch finals and you didn't even say anything about it. You didn't even say congratulations! You never come to my double Dutch competitions and you never spend time with Cameron. This isn't just about you! It's about *us*!" I cry. "I'm going to be at Madison Square Garden and if you don't show up, I will never . . ."

Beep! "Thank you for your message. Good-bye," the machine says. *Uuuugh!* I can't stop crying. I just want us to be together, a family like Sally's. Is that so difficult? I lie on the bed, crying and writing like crazy in my diary. I wonder if they're going to even care about how I feel. I wish I could stop caring, but I just can't.

By morning I feel a little relieved, even though the voice mail cut me off. I don't even know if they got the message, but for now I have to put my parents in the back of my mind. I have the big double Dutch show, and I don't want my new team to see my sad side. We are on our way, and I won't let anything take away how happy I am about it, not even them.

Cameron is driving back with my aunt and uncle and cousins. They would take a flight, but my uncle Larry has a terrible fear of flying. I have no idea how he is an army veteran and still hasn't gotten over his fear. As for me, our sponsors bought us all first-class tickets and got us a hotel right in the middle of Times Square! As long as I've lived in New York, I've never stayed in a Manhattan hotel. I guess sponsors are a good thing, because I'm not just going home, I'm going home in style! I'll also be competing in the double Dutch competition I've been dreaming about since I was like eight years old. Now I have a bigger team with crazy costumes, an awesome routine, and the best coaches, and best of all, everyone's become really good friends. Even Sally and Ivy are cool again, like "peas and carrots," as they say in the South. I never would have thought I'd be so excited, not in a million years. Well, I shouldn't get too excited; we still have work to put in at Madison Square Garden.

In the morning, the coaches hurry us to get ready because a bus will be there to pick us up outside the hotel. *A bus?* We're only about six blocks from the Garden. *Why don't we just walk?* But when we get to the curb, this huge bus pulls up. "Wow!" the whole team says as it stops right in front of us. The bus is covered in a tropical forest theme or something. *Ah, sponsors, right!* I'm guessing the sponsor logo is for some special water that's supposed to help us stay hydrated. *Cool!* When we climb on, we see other teams all ready to jump. I am amazed to see kids from all over the United States. I can't help but think we look like a can of mixed nuts with sprinkles—all dressed up in fresh gym clothes and anything that sparkles, glitters, or shines. And there are more boys! *What? Now, that's different.* But who cares? They all are about to get smoked by the Carolina Fire Jumpers! *I'm repping North Carolina. Really?*

As we pull away from the curb toward the competition, I wonder if both of my parents are going to be there. I know my aunt and uncle and the boys will be there for Sally, but I don't know about my family. Will my mom and dad make excuses? And if my parents do show up, will they be *together* together or just together?

The bus driver clicks on the sound system, and it gets everyone's attention.

"Welcome to New York City, everyone!" he says, and we all cheer. His heavy New York accent suddenly sounds weird to me. "As I understand it, you guys are on your way to a competition for double Dutch, which, I'll be honest, I didn't know existed." Everyone laughs or boos. *How can you live in New York and not know about the biggest double Dutch contest in the world?* "Ah, what are you gonna do?" He laughs to himself. "But since I was hired to get you guys to Madison Square Garden safe and sound, I want you to sit back and enjoy the ride." He clicks off, then clicks on again. "Oh yeah, but I did remember a song from back in the day. I'll play it for you. It might help you guys get into the mood to jump around." *No, he didn't.* "So take your earplugs out and take a listen to"—*no, he isn't*—"'Double Dutch Bus'!" *Yes, he did.* All of us laugh, but without a doubt we sing along to every word. . . . "There's a double Dutch bus coming down . . ."

We arrive at Madison Square Garden and it's everything I hoped it would be. As teams move between velvet ropes into the entrance of the huge arena, the place is so full of excitement that I can feel it on my face. And with all the cameras flashing from everywhere, I feel like a pop star! People hold up banners and wear T-shirts supporting teams. It looks like people brought everyone in their family, including Grandma and Grandpa. I look around for my family. I don't see any of them, but I do see Ms. Jackson! I run and catch her off guard with a big hug.

"Well, well, well, look who made it to nationals," Ms. Jackson says as we both smile. Seeing her after all this time makes me realize how much I look up to her. "How was your summer?"

"It was great." I giggle. "I mean, I'm here, aren't I?" It's like I suddenly forgot about how much we got on each other's nerves.

"That doesn't surprise me." Ms. Jackson stares a bit. "I knew you could." I just smile and hug her again. I miss her being my coach. It's really because of her keeping me in check that I'm here. Then I spot my New York friends right behind her, looking at me like I'm crazy. I let Ms. Jackson go and I'm over to them in a flash.

"Oh my gosh!" I yell as we all hug. "This is crazy! You made it!"

"Of course we did," Mimi says. "You didn't think we'd let you down, did you?"

"Not for one minute!" I'm so happy to see them.

"Look at your hair!" Nikki says. "It looks so pretty." Before I can even thank her, Eva interrupts.

"But we had to replace you," Eva says, pointing to a boy with big, curly hair. *Hold up, needle scratch.*

"What?" I ask. "Who's that?"

"Jesse," Nikki says with a glimmer in her eye. "And he's really good."

"Well, we'll see about that," I say.

"We also had to add two more turners," Eva says with raised eyebrows. "I'm jumping this time." I look over to see two other girls, who wave when they see me looking. I wonder a moment about Jesse and if he's as good as me, good enough to beat my new team. *Competitor mode sets in.*

"Don't worry," Mimi says. "When you get back home we'll start practicing for the Holiday Classic, since you'll be back on our team." I don't have time to think about that. I'm still eyeing curly-top Jesse.

"Okay, sounds cool," I respond quickly.

"So who's your team?" says Eva as she sizes us up.

I snap back to reality. "Oh, uh, these are the Fire Jumpers." There are confused expressions on my friends' faces as they take a look at the mixed group of girls from North Carolina. Everyone waves politely. "And this is my cousin Sally. She is awesome in the ropes, you guys."

"Awesome?" Eva squints. "Is that like your new word?" I roll my eyes.

"So this is the same cousin Sally you said you . . . ," starts Nikki.

"Nice to meet you, Sally." Mimi waves and nudges Eva.

"Hi, nice to meet you," says Sally.

"She's the reason for the new hair, and we're cool now," I say to clear things up for them. "I'll fill you in later."

"Well, I hope you brought your A game, because we came up with a whole new routine," Eva taunts. *Is she really going there?*

"Yeah, Jesse gave us some good ideas." Nikki beams again, then beckons to Jesse. He trots over confidently. Okay, he's cute, but not cuter than my Charlie. "Jesse, this is Kayla."

" 'Ey, what's up?" Jesse says with a nice, firm handshake. "I've heard so much about you."

"Welcome to the Jets," I say, still checking him out carefully. "I mean, their team, for now at least."

"Uh, yeah," Eva says with a smirk. "About the name . . . we're now the BK Crazy Legs." They all jump and criss-cross their legs and pump their arms and chant.

"Turn down for what?" they yell, and laugh. I smile but suddenly feel like I've missed something that happened with my friends this summer.

"That's cool!" I say, trying to hide my feelings.

"Come on, ladies!" Coach Kirsten yells. "We've gotta get signed in."

"Have you seen my parents?" I ask my homegirls before we're shoved off. They just shake their heads and give me weird looks, since they probably can't remember the last time my parents showed up to anything.

"Good luck!" Mimi yells.

"Yeah, good luck." I wave back.

"I guess we'll see you out on the floor," Eva says with that beast-mode look in her eye. I get it, because I'm right there with her.

As if things couldn't get crazier this summer, now I'm competing against my own friends. Well, no matter what happens, it's game time. May the best team win!

The Moment When . . .

As soon as I step into the arena, my stomach drops like I'm on a four-story roller coaster. *Wow!* Madison Square Garden. *I'm really here!* I've been here once before to see the circus, but today all eyes will be on us. I will definitely have to write this down in my diary because this is one day—well, one *summer*—I don't ever want to forget.

"Close your mouth. You're drawing flies," Melissa jokes.

"You don't understand," I say, still amazed. "I've always dreamt of this moment and now I'm here. This is just crazy."

"Okay, listen up, girls," says Coach Kirsten. "You're going to see a lot of great competition out there, but don't let that shake your confidence or let anyone get in your head." She looks to Gabriella as if Gabriella tried to intimidate her once. I don't know how those two managed to become friends, but maybe it's something that comes with getting older. Or maybe they both understand that we've all become friends for the love of double Dutch, and they get our competitiveness.

"You guys have worked hard, and now all you have to do is stay focused and stick to the routine," adds Coach Gabriella.

"What if we mess up? What if something happens?" Brie panics.

"Well, well, well, look who's nervous," teases Melissa. "This is my first time and I can't wait to get out there and show them how awesome we are!"

"Great attitude, Mel," encourages Coach Gabriella.

"Yeah, we're not going to mess up! Don't even say that!" Tina adds.

"I have to go to the bathroom," Ivy says nervously. "Do I have time?"

"Really? Are you serious?" asks Sally. I giggle. *Sally pulled the same thing not too long ago.* "This is not funny, Kayla!"

"It's just that they've acted like they were so big and bad in their small little town," I say.

"Don't be such a jerk, Kayla," Brie retorts.

"I'm not being a jerk! You guys don't make any sense. You were mad at my cousin because she messed up your chances to get here, and now you're scared? Welcome to the big leagues, Belles. It's time to step up!"

Brie sulks. "I just didn't know it was going to be like this!" she admits. "Look at these teams! Look at this place!" She crosses her arms and scrunches up her face like she's going to cry. Coach Gabriella shoots me a sideways look.

"Okay, I'm sorry," I apologize. "But this is no time to chicken out. We're competing against the best jumpers in the country, including my team from Brooklyn—my friends—and they're great. But as much as I don't want to admit it, my new team is amazing and our routine is the best I've ever been a part of. We can do this."

"All right, then! Are we ready?" Gabriella screams.

Kirsten throws her hand out to the center. "Fire Jumpers on three! One-two-three!" she yells.

"Fire Jumpers!" we all scream. Ivy tugs on Kirsten. She still has to go to the bathroom.

"Unfortunately, Ivy, you're going to settle down and hold it," says Kirsten. "After compulsory, then you can go." Ivy winces, but it seems Kirsten has seen her act like this before. Something tells me she's the type who will pee on herself just for attention.

Before we can finish stretching, the National Double

Dutch Jump-off begins. My stomach is in knots, but I put in my earbuds and play my favorite beast-mode song to get in the zone. I start speed-jumping with an imaginary rope while Sally and Tina are jumping single ropes to warm up. Melissa is warming up by doing push-ups. *Wow! And she sure can do them perfectly.* Brie is trying to stay distracted by jumping around with her eyes closed and earbuds in. Ivy . . . well, she's pacing.

Every now and then I peek up to see where we are in the order of teams. It looks like the six- to eleven-year-olds are up first. *They're so cute.* I remember when I started jumping double Dutch. I was as serious about it then as I am now, and I still hold the record for the most jumps in a minute in that age group.

Today, since I don't have the solo, the least I can do is top my own record and put my new team ahead in the scores. We're up next! I look up for my mom and dad but still see only my uncle, aunt, cousins, and Cameron. I also see my friends on their feet, cheering us on. I'm so happy they came, but where are my parents?

We take the floor to pass the compulsory test. Even though everyone takes this part lightly because it's so easy, if you don't pass, you don't move on to the next phases: speed and fusion. So if we make one little mistake, all the practices, arguing, and rivalry will be for nothing. With two new jumpers, I am praying hard . . . on the inside.

As we pick up the ropes, I squint at Ivy as if to say, *You better not mess up.*

Sally and I turn first while Brie and Ivy jump to lift their legs high and then put one foot over the other, hop around on one foot, and jump out. Seamless. While the ropes are still turning, Brie and Ivy take them from us and turn for Tina and Melissa. I'm a little nervous because Tina wasn't allowed to have her earbuds this time. Tina gives me and Sally a reassuring nod, while Melissa keeps her eyes focused on the ropes. As they get going, they count every step together. Hey, whatever works, do it! And they do. Perfect. *Thank goodness!* Then they turn for me and Sally, and without fail we complete the compulsory test. *Piece. Of. Cake!*

I look up. No Mom and Dad. Again, I try to hide the disappointment, but it's too hard. I can't help thinking that they just don't care about how much this moment means to me. How could they not show up? Why would they do this to me? I'm here! *I'm here, at Madison Square Garden!* As always, I'll just bury the hurt under my feet, stomping out the pain with each fast and furious step I take.

But first I watch the speed competition, especially Jesse, the new guy. I hear a judge say, "Three thirty-five, a new record!" *Wow! Okay.* I take one last look in hopes that my mom and dad finally showed up, but I don't see them.

I concentrate on what I have to do. The arena quiets as soon as I take the floor for the speed test. It's cool that the judges recognize me and add an extra judge to count. They must know that I hold the novice record. I give Sally and Melissa my game face.

"You can do this, cuz," Sally says before the ropes. I nod without saying a word, but it feels great to hear her say something encouraging. *Thanks.* Out of the corner of my eye, I see two of the judges hunch over to stare at the center of the ropes, where they continuously tip-tap the hardwood floors. They have to simultaneously press the tiny hand counters with their thumbs every time my left foot hits the ground. I'm happy they are wearing glasses. My feet are burning to smoke up the hardwood at Madison Square Garden. On the whistle, I float between the ropes like there's wind underneath my wings, but as soon as my left foot hits the ground, I get to work. My feet tap the floor ever so lightly while beads of sweat form on my forehead. And although I should concentrate on my speed, my mind begins to wander off to everything that happened this summer.

If there is anything I learned from the trip down south, it's that I will be learning about people, and how to deal with different people, all the time. How to get along, how to let things be so they work themselves out, and how to hope for things to go my way but not be disappointed if they don't. I've learned I'm not perfect and I shouldn't expect anyone else to be: not Sally, not her friends, not my friends, not anyone. And most of all, I learned that no matter what the outcome may be with my parents, they are going to do whatever is good for them, and Cameron and I will have to be okay with it. Faster and faster my feet skip the ropes as I think more and more about my parents. I even stretch out my hands to tell Sally and Melissa to turn faster! I want my parents to stay together. *Is that too much to ask?* Faster. I don't care what Charlie says; I want them to stay together. *I don't want two families. I don't want to have to travel back and forth. Am I being selfish, or is this normal? Why aren't they here? Faster. Why don't they know how much this means to me? I can't jump any faster! They act like they love me, but they don't! They don't love me!* Tears add to my sweat as I give it my all, jumping faster and faster.

"*Time!*" the judge calls. I jump out of the ropes and slump with my hands on my knees. I can't stop crying. The judges agree quickly on the number: "Three seventy-seven! We have a new record!"

"That was excellent!" Sally yells. Melissa is huffing and puffing as much as I am as I pace. It's her first time and she did it.

"That's gotta be . . . some kind . . . of record or something," Melissa pants. I guess she didn't get it. That *is* the new record, and my parents missed it! Gabriella quickly runs over to me.

"Are you okay?" she asks as she shoves a towel in my face. I nod and wipe my face and pretend I'm okay. She stares at me a moment, then pulls me by the hand and gets in my face. "I don't know what's going on with you, but you were amazing out there! Fusion is up next, so I'm going to need you to pull it together. We can do this! Yes?" I nod. The fierce competitor in Gabriella shows her face. If I wasn't afraid of her before, I might be now. Gabriella doesn't pull any punches. She wants to win like she has something to prove. Man, she's tough, but she's right. *I have to get it together.* I take in a deep breath and blow it out like a blowfish, but before I can move, I hear, *"Kayla!"* I look up and it's my mom and dad! They're here!

"We saw you, baby!" my mom yells. "You were fantastic!"

"That's my girl!" yells my dad.

The smile on my face can't get any bigger. Waving to them isn't enough. I run over and hug them both so tight.

"Baby, you were amazing!" my mom says, hugging me. "I'm so proud of you!"

"I love you, Mommy! Daddy! I'm so glad you're here!" I cry.

"We're here, baby," Dad tells me. "Stop crying. We're all right." He stares into my eyes for a moment as if he's answering the question in my voice mail. My mom grabs my sweaty face, kisses my cheek, and looks into my eyes.

"Everything's okay, sweetie," Mom says. "Everything's going to be good, okay?" I can't help the tears falling from my eyes. I don't know if what she's saying is true and that we'll be okay forever, but right now I want to believe her so bad. Yes, I want everything to be okay. I hug both of them again tightly.

"Come on, Kayla!" my team screams at me. I don't want to let go of my parents, but I have to. I quickly get back to the floor—my energy is back to a hundred! I'm ready to crush it!

Luckily, the Jets—well, the new BK Crazy Legs, aka my friends—are called on before us. Their routine is really hot! Honestly, I'm not shocked, but I am curious about Jesse and what is so special about him that they put him on the team. As I watch, I see him jump single rope like no one before. Okay, now I see. I don't think anyone has seen quadruple rotations with acrobatics in a single rope. He's springing up like he's jumping rope on a trampoline. He is amazing! The only thing, though, is he's not doing the tricks with double ropes, so they won't count. *Ugh!* My team still needs me. Even though they might have lost points during time on the single rope, BK Crazy Legs is the team to beat. *Ugh, again!* This is so hard. Although I love my home team, I don't want to let down my new team. *What am I gonna do?* I just have to do what I have to do.

We're up, and as soon as we get in our places we realize Ivy is missing! She's been in the restroom way too long.

"Go on!" urges Coach Kirsten. "Maybe she's lost. I'll try to find her. Go!"

Gabriella sets up our ropes as we slip into our second costumes: electric jumpsuits. Then she gives the DJ a thumbs-up.

The audience seems eager to see something. The music starts, and people get into it. It's a hot mix of the latest hip-hop and techno. My cousin Marc hooked it up for us. Brie and Melissa turn the ropes. Suddenly the lights go out, but our ropes glow in the dark and our suits are made with lights that create crazy patterns along with the beat. It's some really cool app Marc and Gabriella have been working on. The crowd goes crazy for it! *It looks incredible!* Sally and Tina do a dance while I float in and out of the ropes, jumping with excitement in my step! *My parents are watching!*

"Sally, get ready!" Gabriella yells from the sideline. "Ivy is MIA. You do the solo!"

Sally gets that frightened look on her face.

"Sally!" I yell as she snaps out of it. "You got this!"

She cracks a smile. "I know," she says confidently. *Redemption time.*

Melissa and Brie wiggle the ropes while Sally, Tina, and I do the dance portion. Brie and Melissa put down the ropes and join us in the dance for a few seconds, then pick up and get back to turning. Tina and I do a doubles routine. High kicks, leapfrog, and we both do a four-legged spider spin. It's crazy, but we do it without a glitch. Sally has turned off her suit and runs to one end of the court. She turns her suit back on. As soon as Tina and I exit the ropes, Sally does three backflips and cartwheels into the ropes. *Yes!* Tina and I take the ropes to turn for Sally's solo. *She's not frozen this time!* Seconds later, a sixth jumpsuit that glows in the dark comes flipping across the stage. The crowd goes wild! It's Ivy!

"Move down!" Ivy yells to Sally. Sally hesitates for a few seconds. Maybe this is payback. "Come on! We can do it together." Sally moves down. Ivy jumps in and the crowd cheers. Tina and I keep an eye on their every move so we don't mess up the ropes. Sally jumps out and lets Ivy have her moment. Brie and Melissa take over the ropes while Tina, Sally, and I dance more out of happiness than a routine. Ivy does a spectacular forward flip, then a double backflip and a slip. Tina and I grab a rope end from Brie and Melissa, and we do a pinwheel routine while Ivy and Sally jump through, and in seconds, we finish with a bang! The crowd is on their feet! Even my friends cheer for us. I can't believe it. *We did it!*

· · ·

That night, walking into my own bedroom with a double Dutch trophy that reads 1ST PLACE is the best feeling in the whole world. Then again, my parents don't exactly explain to me that they are back together, but the fact that they are hugging and kissing each other means they don't have to say it officially. Maybe that would jinx things.

I feel pretty silly, thinking my parents didn't love me. Remembering all the things they taught me my whole life is what got me through this summer. And as much as I hate to admit it, I had the best summer of my life. As I lie on my bed wondering if it was all a dream, I glance at my trophy again. *Nope, it was all real.* I grab my suitcase and dig out my diary. I definitely have to recount every moment of this day. It's one I never want to forget.

Knock, knock!

"Come in!" I say as I bury my diary under a pillow. I'm not ready to tell my mother about the kiss. My mom *and* dad are at the door.

"Hey, baby girl," my dad says. "We're real proud of you, sweetie, and we wanted to thank you for taking good care of yourself and your brother this summer." I can only smile.

"You're growing up so beautifully, baby," Mom says.

"And thank you for being honest with us about how you feel. You sounded really upset in your voice mail, and it made us realize that we really haven't been paying much attention to you and your brother. And we're sorry, honey."

"I promise you, we're going to do better," Daddy chimes in. "I mean that." I hope he's being honest.

"We may not be perfect, but you and Cam mean the world to your dad and me," Mommy says. "I hope you can forgive us?" I nod and hug her tight.

"And," my dad says as he pulls a box from behind his back, "we got you a little something." *What?* Is that what I think it is?

"Oh my . . . ," I gasp. I tear open the box. It's a phone!

"Now, be responsible with it, honey," my mom says.

"That means no talking on it all day and night," my dad says. "Or letting it distract you at school. And if you lose it—oh well. You'll have to get the next one on your own."

"Johnnie!" My mom taps him. "Enjoy it, baby. You deserve it."

"Good night, baby girl," my dad says as he closes the door. I'm not really sure if he says anything after that, because once I turn on the phone, I find one number in the back of my diary I've been wanting to call ever since I've been back. I dial.

"Hello, Kayla from BK," a voice says.

"How'd you know it was me?" I melt.

"Uh, area code," Charlie says jokingly. "So tell me, what's good?"

"Nothing, um, everything," I stutter. "I don't even know where to begin."

"How about I start?" Charlie asks.

"Okay, go ahead," I say.

"I'll be in New York for Christmas," says Charlie.

I'm speechless. *Butterflies.*

Acknowledgments

*W*hen asked whom I'd like to acknowledge, so many names and faces flooded my mind. I welled up as if I'd been asked to read my acceptance speech for an Academy Award. And since I might forget a few names when I do receive an Oscar or an Emmy—totally dreaming—I thought I'd take this opportunity to express my deepest gratitude to everyone who contributed to this novel by way of support, inspiration, influence, or sheer presence in my life and career. It took a village to raise this child of the arts, so to all the following people, I give you my sincerest thanks.

Charlie S. Dannelly II, my husband, my love, my rock, thank you for not judging me as I walked around the house in my pajamas all day, toiling over my manuscript. Your generous, unwavering belief in me is like delicious coffee in my cup. It warms and motivates me, and God knows I couldn't do without it.

For my parents, Gloria and Frank Spicer, thank you for your love and for teaching me the true meaning of fortitude. By your example I've learned to get up when I fall, accept my mistakes, and press on. I can't thank you enough for getting back up.

Most special thanks to my brother Frank "Pop" Spicer Jr., for your consistent encouragement and for having my back since day one of my journey, and to my fun-loving sister Yvette Spicer-Jackson, for every braid you put in my hair, for every party you've thrown on my behalf, and for showing me the ropes by teaching how to—1 up 2-3-4-5-6-7-8-9! Pop and Yvette, your influence on my life is bigger than you might realize. There's a piece of you in everything I do.

For my amazing grandmother, Tomasita Rosario—had it not been for your sacrifice, I don't know if any of my dreams would have come true. Thank you so much for teaching me how to pray, your greatest gift. I love you, Grammy!

To my precious in-laws, Senator Charlie S. Dannelly and Rose Dannelly, for your love and support and for helping me fall in love with Charlotte, North Carolina.

Darrell Miller, Esq., thank you for taking me on as a client more than twenty years ago. You inspire me.

To my agent, Regina Brooks, and her assistant, Jocquelle S. Caiby, and Team Serendipity Agency, thank you for all your hard work. I'm happy to be your client!

Especially to the incredible senior editor at Penguin Random House, Diane Landolf, thank you for encouraging me to explore the smallest details that made huge differences in every draft. If I'm revered as a rock-star author, it's because of you.

For my mentors and dynamic authors Jeff Rivera (my cousin), L. Divine, and Cecil Castellucci, thank you all for your awesome advice.

For Team Spicerack Productions Inc., George Blake, Marlene Sharp, Yolonda Brinkley, Sonia Evans, and Angela McCrae, thank you for your constant support. You guys are the best! And my interns Allison P. Jackson (my niece), Morgan Tucker, and Ameerah Holiday, for your noteworthy thoughts. Also to Peggy Iafrate with Strega Marketing for jumping aboard and making magic happen.

For the entire Spicer and Perez family, especially my dearest cousins Patricia Tucker and Barbara Commissiong, with whom I've spent fun, unforgettable summers on Long Island. To Eddie Carson, Mark Thomas, Fred Watson, Michael Francis, Monique Perez-Jones, and Tico Perez, you guys made life so much sweeter growing up as a teen from the concrete jungle of New York City. I thank you all for simply being you.

To my brothers Anthony Spicer and Eric Spicer and my sister Elizabeth Spicer-France, thank you for allowing me to be a part of your life. And, Liz, thank you for Tiger. He's the best furry writing partner anyone could have.

To my godparents, Eitelle and Franklin Ford—I don't

know where I'd be without your love and support at every stage of my career. To my second moms and spiritual teachers, Odaris Jordan, Joyce Payne, Dr. Virginia Flintall, and Christine LeMaire, your words of wisdom and examples of grace and courage carry me to this day.

For Tony Jackson and Anthony Jackson Jr., Elizabeth Leite, Elza and Clai Rocha, Gail and Amari Sealy, Cynthia and Charles Hernandez, and Lee and Betty Collins, your love and support are a blessing in my life.

For Samm-Art Williams, for deeming me worthy of a shot at Hollywood. I hope I've made you proud. Thank you to Dr. Valeria Sedlak, my English professor, and Mrs. Edna Peschel, my seventh-grade English teacher, who gave me words of encouragement that will forever be emblazoned on my heart.

To the late David Walker for starting the National Double Dutch League, and to Lauren Walker and double Dutchers everywhere who carry on his legacy.

To the best of my friends and the worst of my bullies, thank you for bringing out the best in me and giving me reason to spread love through #lovedoubledutch and #iamgirlstrong.

In loving memory of my aunt Jean Francis. Her legacy lives on in everyone who ate at her table.

Above all, to the Almighty Creator, from whom all blessings flow, to You be the glory.